THIRTEEN OFFERINGS

STORIES OF ITHIRIA

APRIL WAHLIN

DEDICATION

This book is dedicated to everyone who has let me sit with my computer to rant about the fictional characters running rampant in my imagination. Especially to all the ADs and PAs who let me write for numerous hours while on set.

This is dedicated to every storyteller who has had the gumption to get their work out there and seen, without whom I might not have had the inspiration for my own worlds.

To my mother, who has wanted nothing more for me than to do whatever it is I love to do.

To my friends, who keep me sane and have no problem following me on whatever random endeavor I come up with. And to my man who is a great source of support and inspiration.

To my editor, who has had amazing patience and encouraging words for me. Your patience and input are beyond valuable.

To every person who took a chance on picking up this work and taking time out of their day to spend a moment with my creations.

Above all, this is dedicated to everyone who has believed in me and encouraged me to write—for no good reason other than having listened to me ramble madly for any length of time.

Thank you all!

CONTENTS

THE CENTENNIAL

The streets of Hollywood were wholly unlike the roads of packed dirt and cobbled stones of his homeland. Here, paved trails wound up into little suburban alcoves lined with houses akin to small mansions. Three or four families could comfortably live in any one of them; yet most were owned by single persons.

Patrick looked up to the hazy and dim moon. It would have been a beautiful night, if not for the smoggy air which blew in rough bursts through his dark, shortly cropped hair. It was cold in the land of

Hollywood but this was more than a nighttime chill, uncharacteristically cold. What a time to have cut off his hair—his usual mane would never have permitted the darkly tanned goose bumps now rising on his neck. He adjusted the high collar of his deep brown duster, determined not to let the wind get the better of him.

Though this realm was strange to him, there were elements that resembled his own. This land—this Vacant Realm—was a shrunken, mashed version of his homelands—like a theme park exhibit of a world wonder. It had only seven small continents, yet the intricacies of its continent Europe bore similarities to the Highlands, Industrial Domain, and even his homeland of Old World.

Patrick marveled. How could a land so removed from the rest of the realms mimic so accurately? Every region was separated by vast oceans and great walls of magic. Yet each realm was acutely aware of one another. So unlike this land, floating in its own smoggy haze of delusion.

Passing through pools of light cast from street lamps above, he was somewhat startled when a motorized carriage with bright lanterns roared up the road. The carriage resembled a squat, oversized, monster—the road was hardly wide enough to accommodate its rumbling, bulky frame. The driver, who had written his name garishly across the front, had little care for sharing the street. Whoever this Hummer person was, Patrick did not care to become acquainted. He already missed the Homelands.

Rounding the corner onto the dead-end street that

was Mt. Olympus Drive, Patrick gazed up at its gaudy homes. He had met their owners and could only shake his head at the excessive waste. Scores of people went homeless in this realm, as well as in his own, yet these were homes built for owners who lived here for only a few weeks every decade. Like them, Patrick came for the Social Ball.

For hundreds of years the Vacant Realm had been almost stagnant in progress, but now it seemed newer and stranger each time he crossed its gateway. Even the Industrial Domain, known for its vast machines and T-Coil Technology, had nothing on this land. Here one could effortlessly access a massive information source or contact a person a thousand miles away—without the use of magic—with the slightest touch to a small device.

Coming to the end of the street, he gazed up at the most extravagant estate done out in gold and littered with intricately carved statues—a home fit for the king of Mount Olympus Drive. But this was not his destination.

Out of the corner of his eye, Patrick caught sight of the weed-infested yard set back a hundred yards from the main road. It was easy enough to ignore if you weren't looking for it. In fact, a curse placed on the yard made it difficult for most people to even enter. However, Patrick knew its tricks.

As he passed through the rickety wooden gate surrounding the shack set into the hill, he heard them—the weeds. Not just there to deter passersby, they were a defense mechanism which sprang up to snag his feet.

Quickly, Patrick chanted a counter spell to hinder their progress. They were halfway up his leg when he heard the rusty hinges of the front door squeal.

"Need assistance?" came a deeply accented voice.

The Celt standing in the shack's doorway shared Patrick's height and coloring, but wore his hair in ropy dreadlocks that hung nearly to his elbows. Wrapped in faded layers, he looked as unkempt and foreboding as the home itself.

With a wave of his hand, the man dismissed the snaring weeds, sending them back to their various corners of the yard.

Shaking the soil from his boots, Patrick made his way to the door.

"It's about time you showed."

"Good to see you too, Angus," Patrick replied.

Angus had never been good with—well, anything resembling manners.

"What's it been? A hundred years?" Angus smirked.

"No, no. I saw you a few leap years back, at the Ball."

"Ahhh, yes. How could I forget?"

"Meg," they said simultaneously. The hostess of the Ball was a legendary beauty and a favorite of the two brothers.

"I look forward to coercing a dance out of her at the ball tomorrow," Angus mused.

"She is all yours this time. My eye is with the living."

"You're missing out. The undead can be quite beguiling. Well, come in, Brother. Let us get started."

"Always one to get right to it," Patrick said with a smirk, and headed inside.

Angus's home always reminded Patrick of his homeland. It was a home made from the earth itself, a stark contrast to the modern Vacant Realm of motorized carriages and electricity. Despite living in the epicenter of one of the most technologically advanced societies in the world, he lived as he had since the formation of the realms themselves: as a hermit trader. At least Patrick traveled. His brother loved nothing more than to stay in his hovel. He never understood Angus, and after a millennium, he was positive he never would.

They left the crudely constructed entry, making their way to the back of the shed. There the decrepit wooden boards turned to root and dirt tunneling down into the earth.

"Are you sure we shouldn't wait for the others?" Patrick asked as they made their way down into the hidden structure beneath the hill.

"There will only be a couple of us this time. Our absent brothers will be of best service where they are. We must keep the balance. That is why I asked you to bring more than the usual offering. There is no need to wait."

Angus paused then and began fussing with a large fuse box sunk into the wall. Patrick thought on the changes to their ceremony. For hundreds of years they had been conducting the Centennial. They always met in the Vacant realm, every brother, late though they may be. Starting without them seemed—wrong.

"Come now. I'm sure we can hold off just little longer. Our brothers have never been timely."

"This is different," Angus replied solemnly.

"Different? We have been conducting this ceremony for millennia. What could possibly be different now?"

"The Fates."

"The Fates?" Patrick asked in shock. "What do they want?"

"I don't know but it has something to do with the disturbances."

Patrick stood stunned. He had heard about the trouble with magical alloys in other realms, even his own had been affected, but he never imagined it would involve the Fates. The last time they received interference the Great Depression happened, and it was far more depressing for the lands outside the Vacant Realm. When the Fates intervened, it was never a good sign.

"We cannot risk a mistake because of our brothers' tardiness," Angus continued. "You remember what happened the last time we failed to complete the Centennial."

"Yes, but we survived the Dark Ages and all was righted—for the most part."

Angus gave his brother a skeptical glare. "Banon will see that our absent brothers receive their gifts. I trust him to do that much. As for the ceremony, our attending brothers assured me that we will have the thirteen offerings needed. I have a very old offering from before the land break, an ancient elemental."

Patrick nodded. "That is a rare gem."

The older the offering, the more power it summoned from the ceremony. From what Angus was saying, it seemed like they could use all the strength they could get.

"How fares things in Old World?"

"The magical alloys are noticeably weakening," Patrick told him dismally. "There have been a few mining catastrophes as a result. Uncovered some dangerous magic in the dwarven mines. What of this land?"

"The discord is not yet prevalent in the Vacant Realm. I doubt anyone aside from myself and a few of the stronger entities have even picked up on it. You noticed the strong winds on the way here?"

"That was peculiar for this area," Patrick replied.

"The elemental magic here is not strong enough to cause destruction, but something is stirring. I have taken time away from the affairs of the Vacant Realm to conduct this meeting. I need the strength."

"Are you sure it's safe here?" Patrick asked with a wary eye.

"If something is happening to the magical compounds, we'll be the last afflicted," Angus assured him.

Patrick shook his head. "My sight is not as far reaching as your own. I have to ask—do you think they are waking?"

Angus sighed heavily. "It has been a millennia. I don't see why now, but it's hard to tell. If they do, not even this land will be safe."

It was grave news, confirming Patrick's worst fears.

There were ancient creatures that slept in the world, deep within its very core, forgotten by most. Even Zeus himself had never seen these creatures. While they sleep, Ithiria drives on, thriving, growing. But if they were disturbed, the world as they know it could cease to exist. This was their purpose, this was the brothers' task in the Centennial, to provide the ancients with an offering to keep them appeased. In return, the brothers received the power to keep and watch over the lands. To protect the balance.

"How fares the Vacant Realm?" Patrick asked, hoping for a less worrisome conversation, but no such luck.

"Not peaceful. We have had an uprising in the supernatural community."

"A civil war?"

"Of sorts. Some of the creatures here wish to stay hidden from the non-magic population while others want to drop the veil completely—which would be chaos if not handled tactfully." Angus's voice was surly. "I've had to take a more prominent role in their dealings here."

"I thought it was uncharacteristically quiet when I arrived. What happened?"

"For now the veil has been kept, but we stand in an uneasy limbo."

"Let us speak of merrier things," Patrick suggested

as he followed his brother down the winding dirt tunnels.

They passed walls lined with weaponry, barrels of ingredients, and ominously hissing baskets. Angus's housekeeping was lackluster at best. Even with infinite space, there always seemed to be a clutter.

Winding down the twisting hallways of the anthill Angus called home, they descended deep into the base of the Hollywood hills.

Finally, they came to an ornately carved wooden door covered in figures and ancient depictions. A musty draft of air rushed from the great room within as Angus pulled open the door.

This room was not cluttered like the others—it was a place of offering and seeing. There, as always, sat the massive round wooden table surrounded by high-backed chairs formed from twisting roots running deep into the earth below. The table was fashioned from the stump of one of the oldest trees in the land which, like the chairs, had roots running into the earth—to its very core.

This stump was the base of his brother's connection with the Vacant Realm.

In the center of the table an enormous crystalline ball sat cradled in intricately twisting roots. The sphere's smoky black surface beckoned the viewer to see through its mystic eye. Straight into the soul of Ithiria.

This place was vast, and felt empty. In fact the whole hovel his brother lived in felt empty. Angus was always a home body but he couldn't help feeling that he hadn't had friendly company in some time.

"I hate to see you alone like this," said Patrick, breaking the silence of the still room.

"After my last wife, I suppose I've needed some time to myself."

"That was over a hundred years ago."

"It was a very taxing relationship." Angus's chuckle was dark. "How are you and Beau?"

Patrick should have known his brother would turn the personal spotlight back on him. "Well, I haven't seen her in a couple years, but we are nearing our triennial fair. A reuniting could be in our future."

"I'm glad to hear it," Angus said and smiled. "Well, now that we're settled, we should get to it."

"I don't see why not. The others will show up when they're good and ready, as they always do."

"You first, Brother. Mine is—on the darker side."

"No wonder, with the company you keep."

Angus snorted. "You keep the same sort of friends. Are you not acquainted with a werefeline and several witches?"

"Yes, but our community is different. Here, the supernaturals are repressed and hidden. They are more dangerous."

Angus huffed in disagreement. "Let us continue. The night wears on."

"I will begin then," Patrick replied.

Angus nodded and then both brothers bowed their heads.

Lifting his head a moment later, Patrick stared into the black eye of the ancient table, his own eyes growing opaque as they misted over.

"We Watchers of this land bring offerings for you, great Life Giver, tales from our wanderings and impartial dealings in this world. We who derive tales from all we see and touch, ask your favor. To keep the Eternal Father sleeping, and to help us keep balance in this immortal existence. We beseech you to take hold of these objects and know that which only such an object could know, their boundless travels, the marvels they've witnessed, the feel of the countless hands through which they've passed. In thanks and everlasting gratitude, we begin."

From his coat pocket, Patrick pulled a hefty, foot-long rod made of candy cane.

"I offer the strife of a great witch of Old World. A powerful being attempting to keep balance in her life's dealings and withstand the falsehoods inflicted by neighbors. I bring this cane of sugar, made by her own hand, in the wake of her dismay."

With that, Patrick placed the great candied cane on the table before the crystal ball which glowed ominously. The cane began to spark and boil, losing form and liquefying, as it was slowly absorbed by the great table—becoming one with the waiting roots below.

THE GINGERBREAD WITCH

M issy sat in the living room of her gingerbread home watching her son sink his fangs into a toy truck. She had never had this problem with her daughters. Then again, *their* father had been a sorcerer, not a scientist. Her current husband was a good man and a brilliant scientist. However, she wished he'd mentioned his family's genetic "quirk" before they'd had a child together. The oddity had missed her husband entirely and hit her son full force.

Puberty was not going to be fun.

She sighed as her little boy swallowed the rest of his masticated tinker toy. No matter how much she fed him, he never seemed satisfied. The kid was no bigger than a dwarf, but could somehow manage to eat an entire roast duck and still have room for dessert. At least living in a house made of gingerbread provided her with extra food.

Missy sat back and cackled unexpectedly. Irritated, she put her fingers to her temples. Missy had had this awkward version of Tourette's since she could remember, yet it never ceased to aggravate her. However, annoyance and frustration were feelings she was all too familiar with lately. She groaned as she thought back on the last year of her life. It hadn't been good. Her husband was off researching some experiment, her daughter was away on the school extension trip, and her experiments to correct her Tourette's consistently resulted in altering her skin color. Today she was a dark lime—though she had to admit, it was a far sight better than the canary yellow of the day before.

The throbbing in Missy's temples had just begun to subside when the door chimes interrupted her calm.

"What now?" Missy grumbled, then cackled, and got up to answer the door.

She really needed to check her crystal ball more often; Missy was *not* in the mood for visitors. Looking through the small sugar-glass window, she was surprised to find Genevieve Goose standing on her apple-red, hard-candy porch. When she opened the door, the pleasantly rounded woman looked up through little circular bifocals and smiled tentatively with round, rosy cheeks.

"Hello, Miss Wicked. I need to speak with you, if you have a moment." Genevieve's greeting was politely formal.

"What a pleasant surprise. By all means, come in."

Missy let out a sigh as they settled onto her couch. This wasn't a wholly unexpected visit, and from the look on Genevieve's face, she was not the bearer of good news.

"I think you know why I'm here, Miss Wicked."

"Missy," she corrected, letting out a loud cackle. Genevieve jumped slightly but continued. It wasn't her first trip to Missy's house. "I'm here on government business. I think it will be easier if we keep this formal."

"If you insist, Ms. Goose."

"Thank you." She nodded and took a deep breath. "It's about those children you sent away a few months back. They've been making some rather...wild claims about you."

"Yes, the rumor mill has trickled back to me."

"Then you are aware of their accusations?"

"Yes. They're ridiculous! I would never *eat* a child."

"*I* know that, Miss Wicked."

"You know their background. The children were raised as con artists. Their parents had them begging on the streets before abandoning them. Terrible people!" In her disgust, Missy cackled abruptly.

"Well, the children will be fostered by their uncle in the Industrial Domain."

"Good. Get those two cretins as far away from me as possible. They nearly ate me out of house and home, then blamed me for how fat they got!"

"So, they did accuse you of *fattening them up*?"

"Yes, they got mad when I asked them to do their chores. Which you know I ask of all my tenants since they're staying and eating for free. They are the two laziest children I've ever seen. The little monsters even attacked me when I caught them stealing from my pantry! They nearly shoved me into the oven, which as you know, is huge—I can cook a horse in that thing. Had I actually gone in, I would have been flambéed! That was the last I saw of them and good riddance."

"Yes, well." Genevieve gave a little cough. "They said you threatened to 'serve them up for dinner.'"

Missy's anger burst out unchecked. "One little joke about them being fatter than the turkey we were having for dinner and suddenly I'm a cannibal?"

Genevieve cleared her throat and pushed her glasses farther up the bridge of her nose. "I believe you said," she pulled out a small file and read, "'you two are so round I should serve you up for supper. We would have meat for weeks.'"

Missy let out a high-pitched laugh. The cackles were always worse when she was stressed. "In hindsight, that might not have been the best thing to say, but *honestly*, Genevieve! I have three children of my own. Why would I want to eat those two?"

"I'm sorry about all of this." Genevieve sounded tired. "We thought setting you up out here to help travelers was a wonderful idea. The number of people lost to the Black Woods has seen a substantial decrease in the few years you've been here. Building your house out of sweets to help people find their way was truly a brilliant idea."

"Well, it's just easier for me to maintain," Missy replied modestly. "I'm terrible with thatch and wood, but give me an oven and some sugar and I can produce miracles."

"It was all working out so nicely."

"*Was*? How bad is it, Genevieve?"

Genevieve Goose shifted uncomfortably. "Well... I mean the Cinderella rumors just blew over."

"Oh, not that." Missy groaned. "None of that is true! You can go ask her, or any of my children! I treated her as one of my own. You know what a clean person Cindy is—can't stand to leave a dish unwashed or a floor unswept. She was happy as a clam in my home. But when she told that dullard husband of hers how she spent her time, he took it and ran with it! You know how the Charmings are about my family. They've hated us since grade school."

"I know, but it's the rumors," Genevieve sighed. "Get enough people talking and they can make a saint a sinner. It's all gossip, but that spreads like wildfire in town."

"One of the many reasons I was happy to move out here in the first place."

"Missy..."

Missy took a deep breath, barely able to restrain a nervous cackle. This was it, the really bad news.

"You're going to have to close down the program."

"No!" Missy was stunned. Cutting back her funding or salary she could handle, but being let go all together? "You're firing me? How am I supposed to support my children? My son is only two, his father's always off on some wild goose chase… no joke intended. The Extension Program cost an arm and a leg! This is practically my entire income."

"I'm sorry, Missy. I'll do what I can, but we've been told to disband the project." Genevieve placed a sympathetic hand on Missy's shoulder. The two had been friends in grade school. "You also have to remove the 'Lost and Found' spell you created to guide people here."

"That was a strong piece of magic. It won't be undone easily," Missy groaned.

"You have to, Dear. It's this new government. You know it wouldn't be like this if they had kept the monarchy. Then again, our little program might not even exist if King Richard hadn't stepped down."

No matter how kind Genevieve was, there was no comfort for Missy.

"And…" Genevieve sighed.

"Another *and*?"

"The higher ups have requested you lay low until the brunt of the rumors stop circulating."

"What?!" Missy's cackle was almost a scream. "I'm under House Arrest?"

"Not as bad as all that, but essentially. It shouldn't be too difficult. Amanda is away and there should be more than enough time between now and when your son starts school for this to disappear…You know I would help if I could, but I'm not going to be here much longer. This job is getting to me. I don't think I'll be working for the government anymore."

"No! What are you going to do?" Distressed as she might be, Missy knew how taxing it would be for Genevieve to leave the security of her position.

Genevieve thought a moment and gave a little shrug. "Not sure. I have a teaching degree. I may apply for a position at Legends Primary."

"Well, they would be lucky to have you."

"Thank you, Missy." Genevieve smiled sadly. "Please try not to worry about all this. There's a decent severance package and I'm trying to find another job you can fill in the meantime. You still have your home. You're a very resourceful woman—I know you'll bounce back. You always do."

"Thanks," Missy replied unenthusiastically as she stood to walk her rotund little friend to the door.

"I really am sorry," Genevieve apologized again as she descended the candy steps. Turning back, she flashed Missy a smile. "By the way, that shade of green is lovely on you."

"Thank you." Missy chuckled. "Let's get together for tea sometime soon."

"Only if you make those blueberry crumpets you do so well."

"It's a deal."

Missy waved and watched as Genevieve disappeared from her yard in a gust of magic.

"Great." Missy's forehead hit the door with a soft *thunk*, causing the sugar glass to creak in response. "I really need to start checking my crystal ball." She turned to find her son eating his way through the fruitcake fireplace. "I suppose I could start a candy store." She laughed as she scooped him off the floor. "You'd like that, wouldn't you?"

The robust toddler let out a resonating belch of agreement.

~~~~

The small candy puddle shrank until naught remained but a pinkish-white stain on the table before Patrick. This last remnant faded quickly, as did the luminescent mist which had enveloped his eyes.

"An interesting account of life's hardships."

"Not everything has to be death and destruction," Patrick replied. "I find everyday plights just as relevant as the extraordinary."

"The great oak seems appeased."

"I believe it is now your turn."

"I think we should let our brother go first," Angus replied, leaning back into the frame of his high-backed chair.

Patrick listened. He could faintly hear footsteps coming down the hall. "Killian," he muttered as the resonant thudding of the steps grew louder. "I'm sure he will have a good offering. He always does."

"His land is awash with ancient stories." There was a knock on the chamber door then. "Enter," Angus called and the great door slowly swung open.

"Sorry I am late, brothers," Killian called, closing the door behind him.

A gust of air rushing to escape the room tossed his

gold-brown hair over his shoulder as he headed to the table. Killian was tall and well-built with skin nearly the same golden brown as his eyes and hair, giving him the look of a bronzed statue. He wore a long, flowing jacket the color of storm clouds and a simple dark blue suit beneath, a perfect liaison to the Olympians and ancient creatures of Gods' Grace.

"Have we already begun?" He took the seat to Patrick's right.

"Only just," Angus replied. "Patrick just finished his first."

Killian glanced around at the empty chairs. "I see I am not the only late comer."

"With all that's going on back in the Lands, many of our brothers are held up," Angus said.

"I understand—barely managed to get away myself. Of course, in my land, a little loss of magic is no big issue. However, you know how the inhabitants of Gods' Grace can be. A lot of ancient toddlers, if you ask me. Anyway, I am late due to my accidental transition from the gateway into the king's house. That place is an absolute labyrinth! Ferdinand says 'hello' by the way."

"How is the Minotaur?" Angus asked.

"Living in luxury. The king is hardly ever there and the occasional burglar keeps him plenty entertained."

Angus let out a bark of laughter. "Been meaning to stop by, but time's always slipping away from me."

"It does that to us all," Patrick replied.

"Are you ready, or would you like time to get settled?" Angus asked Killian.

"Always one to get right to it." Killian smirked, earning a chuckle from Patrick. "I suppose there is no reason to delay. I have an old tale as offering, a sad yarn told to me by the Sea God himself."

They all bowed their heads momentarily.

Killian looked to the crystal ball, his gold-brown eyes were now cloudy. "I offer this ancient story, passed on to me by a creature of Gods' Grace: a tale of a monster whose love is vast and true, but stifled by a forbidden curse. I sacrifice this water lily, a relic from the fountain of the once magnificent temple of Athena."

He set the flower before the great crystalline ball where it curled into itself as it began to brown and wilt.

MEDUSA'S REFLECTION

Thais, a small island off the coast of Thasos, was renowned for its beauty and serenity, often attracting visitors from the mainland of Greece. These mainlanders frequently made the watery journey to lounge on the island's white-sand beaches and bathe in its aquamarine waters.

Thais also attracted Greece's most devout, as the island was home to an illustrious temple of Athena which sat back from the pristinely sparkling shore, its grounds covering nearly a quarter of the tiny island. It was said to be the most extraordinary of all Athena's temples—a vision of such wonder, the likes of its magnificence could only be matched in Olympus.

As an infant, Medusa was left on the temple steps and raised in the care of the priestesses. The high priestess favored the child and doted upon the girl as if she were her own. Stern, yet giving in nature, she made sure Medusa was taught the finer nuances of the duties, ceremonies, and songs necessary to worship their beloved goddess.

An astute acolyte, Medusa blossomed into a devoted neophyte and a beautiful, well-mannered child who delighted in singing and playing in the sea. There, in the splendor of the rolling surf, the girl often saw faces in the waves, calm watery faces who welcomed and beckoned her to splash in their midst. But no matter how they called, Medusa would swim no farther than the wake.

The island's inhabitants adored Medusa—cooing over her magnificent golden hair and aquamarine eyes as she passed to collect tributes for their patron goddess. Her beauty grew so with each passing year that the people of Thais gathered in the streets when she walked for alms, just to catch a glimpse of her flowing hair and sparkling gaze. They believed any person lucky enough to catch her eye would be blessed with beauty and good fortune. A more loved, more revered apprentice to Athena's high priestess there never was.

As she aged, Medusa's talents grew to exceed those of any priestess in the temple. Her singing was the most melodious, her dancing the most lithesome, her charms the most beguiling of all the girls. Many said her beauty surpassed even the goddesses of Olympus.

Gods' Harvest was the tiny island's annual festival. The celebration lasted nearly a month, marking the spring's first full lunar cycle. Throughout the year, the islanders eagerly anticipated the ceremonies honoring their beloved goddess. During the great celebration, the people of Thais ate heartily of the island's yield and quenched their thirst with Ambrosia, a sweet wine boldly named after the food of the gods.

The festival concluded with a spectacular night of celebration: the *Goddess's Gala*. The pinnacle of this evening came during their annual Eclipse, which the islanders referred to as the *God's Eye*. It was not a full eclipse, just a brief shadow creeping across the moon's gossamer surface. It could only be seen from the small island and it was said that whosoever dared stare into the eye of the eclipse might catch a glimpse of the gods dancing in Olympus. However, custom dictated all revelers look away the moment the eclipse reached its zenith—if a person was so bold as to stare too long, he or she could be abducted by any god who looked back, or worse, earn the wrath of Athena herself and be struck blind.

In Medusa's sixteenth year, she entered adulthood and could now assist the high priestess in preparing for the *Night of the Goddess* ceremonies. The winds raced along the water, the moonlight danced upon the shore, and the sea rose and fell with a grace never seen anywhere else in Greece. As always, Thais gathered at the great temple for the extravaganza of feasts, performances, libations, and general merriment.

Since the time she was a small girl, Medusa had looked forward to this day. She had prayed to achieve the position of high priestess—thanks to her diligence she had secured the apprenticeship. Medusa had practiced the ceremonies a hundred times in preparation and was resolved to be the most accomplished apprentice in the temple's long and illustrious history.

Finally, in her grand headdress of owl, raven, and robin feathers, Medusa stood atop the sky-scraping steps of the Athenian temple. She was a vision beyond compare in flowing robes of emerald, amethyst, and sapphire. That night, Medusa was officially presented as the high priestess's apprentice. The people were elated: they cheered, threw flowers, and stood in line to hang garlands round her neck.

Medusa shone under the honor and praise. Yet, as the night wore on, and the hour of the eclipse drew nearer, she grew distracted. She was fidgety and anxious, unable to pinpoint the cause of her discomfort. She felt ill at ease as she led the revelers in a song of sea sprites and mysterious waters. As she gave voice to the verses, she felt her eyes drawn to the moon. From then on, she was only half present, as though some force beckoned her gaze toward the sky. As dusk stretched into night, the pull only grew stronger, so strong, the young apprentice could hardly concentrate on the ceremony, the moon demanded her attention. Splendid and full, beautifully poised above the curling sea, its radiance entranced her like never before.

Despite her distraction, Medusa dutifully and gracefully continued to lead the songs and conduct the rituals of the evening. However, in the midst of the wine rituals the high priestess noticed her faltering attentions.

"Child? You are distracted," she said pointedly as they spread flower petals and poured wine at the blessed feet of Athena's great stone likeness.

Medusa looked to the priestess and smiled in embarrassment. "Yes, High Priestess. Perhaps . . . perhaps I am just a little flushed from the excitement." After studying Medusa's face a moment, the priestess offered a comforting smile and turned away, seemingly satisfied with the answer.

Determined not to interrupt the ceremony or incur the dissatisfaction of the high priestess, Medusa took slow breaths to calm her nerves before returning to her duties.

The moon now hung full and robust in the night sky. The Eclipse would soon be upon them. Medusa, her fellow priestesses, and the sea of people below gazed into the face of the radiant moon. Its majestic luster was truly stunning.

Medusa stood as though made of stone, staring helplessly. Silence fell among the islanders as they watched the dark shadow slowly encompass the brilliant white-blue of the moon. The richly glowing face grew smaller and smaller, until naught but the faintest sliver remained.

"The time is here!" the high priestess called, signaling the people of Thais to look away.

The crowd turned as one, shielding their eyes. Medusa's fellow sisters also shifted, bowing their heads. Even the high priestess averted her eyes.

Medusa did not.

Brazenly she stared on, entranced by the faint glimmering whites and pale blues of the moon's silvery face. She knew she should look away, but try as she might, she could not. A force stronger than her young will kept her pliant eyes locked on the moon's shimmering surface.

A brief eternity passed and the eclipse was complete. The blue-white contours were sunk in shadow, the face completely enveloped by the dark. Though the ache in her eyes was terrible, she could not turn. The moon was dense and beautiful in a way she had never known. In this darkness she witnessed an entirely new array of colors, bursting across her vision so quickly she hadn't time to think names for them. The moon was somehow every color at once.

Medusa wondered why such magnificence—such dark splendor—was forbidden. Then, its new onyx surface deepened and took form. She beheld the glimmer of a face, lips curled, smiling down at her. For a moment she thought the visage was Athena's, but it was too masculine. Never before had she seen such an enchanting smile.

Suddenly, Medusa was pulled toward the moon.

For one exquisite moment, exhilaration encompassed her, an elating warmth. As suddenly as it began, the sensation ended and Medusa fell back to the earth.

With a sharp intake of breath, the young priestess's eyes finally closed. When she reopened them, she was surprised to be standing exactly where she had been when the eclipse began. Looking out on the mass of people with heads still reverently bowed, she was dizzy and displaced. Had anyone seen her transgression?

Yes. Someone had. The high priestess stared at Medusa, her face a mask of severity and disapproval—emotions Medusa was unaccustomed to seeing on the priestess. Medusa's blood ran cold; she had been caught violating their customs. Her gaze had betrayed her. The priestess turned to the moon and then to the crowd, in dismissal of Medusa and her abominable act. Arms raised to the crowd, she announced the end of the eclipse in her strong, radiant voice. Medusa joined the islanders in their cheering, but she knew there would be repercussions for her insolence.

As the festivities continued, Medusa tried to distract herself with the wonders of the occasion and the excitement of her new role as apprentice. Unfortunately, neither song nor dance could cheer her completely. Dreading her next encounter with the high priestess, Medusa was more disturbed by the disorientation she'd felt: the sensations of floating, then falling, and the bizarre invigoration. Try as she might, she could not erase the imprint of that prolific smile in the moon's face, the warm rush she'd felt upon seeing the man in the eclipse.

The revelries had finally concluded and the villagers had gone home to dream their mornings away. Medusa placed her feathered headdress in the ceremonial chamber next to that of the high priestess. She had not seen her mentor since the festival ended. Part of her was relieved: another part desperately longed for a glimpse into her thoughts.

Medusa headed quickly to her modest quarters. Turning the corner near her room, her heart sank. The high priestess loomed at her door. Medusa was flooded with a strange sense of dread and relief. She shifted her gaze to the floor and walked forward, already condemned. A rigid hand held the door for Medusa who walked past, not daring to meet her gaze. Brusquely, the priestess followed and shut the door.

"It is a foolish thing, flirting with the gods." The priestess's voice was cutting, direct, and wrought with disappointment.

"Flirting?" Medusa gasped, her face flushed with embarrassment.

"I saw, Medusa!" The priestess hissed in her anger. "True, you are most beautiful, but do not dare think yourself beyond the rules of the gods."

"I would never—"

"I would not have you taken!"

Taken? Medusa thought in confusion.

"We do not look into the eclipse for many reasons, child. The eclipse grants us a window into Olympus.

Mortals are not allowed this intimacy with the gods. With that one look, you may have been blinded. You may have opened yourself to become prey for any god who had a whim to hunt. We are but playthings to the gods, girl. You know this!" the priestess yelled, then quickly calmed herself. "Medusa, you are truly one of Athena's most blessed priestesses. Her rival—Poseidon—would delight in snatching up such a prize."

"I understand," she replied dismally.

"I don't think you do. What if you had called down the wrath of Athena herself? She may cherish your beauty and grace, but she would just as easily delight in the power of destroying it! Just to see those qualities so loved, crushed. You endangered us all." The priestess's yell surprised them both. "These rules cannot be ignored," she continued with a strained calm. "What do you have to say for yourself?"

"I...I don't know what came over me." Tears formed in Medusa's eyes as she attempted to explain the inexplicable restlessness, the unavoidable pull toward the moon's shining eye.

The high priestess sat, her demeanor softening. "The lure of the gods is tempting," she whispered, pushing the thick, golden hair away from Medusa's face. "I cannot express how terrible it would have been if you had been taken. Our mighty goddess would be most displeased."

"Yes, High Priestess." Her reply was no more than a whisper.

"You have done a terrible thing. However, I am

prepared to be lenient on you." Medusa's shoulders relaxed in relief. "No one ever need know of this offense as long as we have no more of this misbehavior. I admit I too have felt the temptation of the gods. Their power and might are wondrous." The priestess sighed wistfully. "You must not be fooled. To pursue the gods would mean to tread an unstable path, riddled with emotion and power we cannot begin to comprehend. We are truly blessed to have the favor of the goddess. It is something we cherish and must never lose. *Anyone* could have witnessed your blasphemy. You do know the punishment?"

"Yes, Priestess," Medusa replied, her thoughts flooding with the horrible stories she had heard of disobedient acolytes.

"Good. Let me never see you disobey again," the priestess warned with a strained smile. "I would be heartbroken to choose other than yourself to take my place. You know I look upon you as my own." With that, she briskly stood. "Now, take your rest and let us forget this incident," she advised, turning to leave.

"I saw something," Medusa blurted suddenly.

The priestess rested her hand on the doorknob to the chamber. "What would that be?"

"A man. In the eclipse. I was pulled upwards. It was dizzying. Then it just . . . stopped."

All warmth evaporated from the priestess as she looked down upon Medusa now. "Let us count you lucky then, that whoever—or whatever—had you, lost interest. You must forget what your eyes have beheld. *Never* speak of this again."

"Yes, ma'am."

"Goodnight then." The door snapped shut behind her.

"Goodnight, High Priestess."

Medusa sat with her thoughts as the dawning light warmed her room. Try as she might, she could not dismiss all she had felt tonight, all she had seen. A deep yearning grew within her, a yearning to see the brilliant face in the moon. She could not shake the curve of that smile, the depth of those eyes.

That night, Medusa's dreams were restless—full of the dark shimmering depths of the moon and the inviting smile therein. She slept fitfully, but after some time found herself on the brink of rest.

As she felt herself begin to drift, a soft voice—a masculine voice—called her name. It was soothing, gentle, and all too alluring. Medusa woke with a start. She sat up in bed, still half in dreams as she looked around the room, listening. There was nothing but the sound of her startled breath. Confused, she lay back, sure it was only a sleepy illusion. No cause to be alarmed.

The voice from her dream was quick to wake her anew. Again she sat straight and listened. When it called once more, she knew it was not the doings of Morpheus, the god of dreams—this voice clearly beckoned from the hallway outside her room. A chill rippled down her spine as she opened the heavy wooden door, cracking it just enough to peer out.

Nothing.

Medusa began to close the door when she heard it again. Flooded with the same exhilaration she'd felt during the eclipse, she did not allow herself to consider her actions as she slipped quietly from her chambers.

There, in the silent hallway a long silvery strand of moonlight cut through the dark, sparkling through the shutters. The beam seared a luminous path to the end of the hall and into the great room of the temple.

Medusa's curiosity urged her forward. She walked alongside the beam, playfully running her fingers through its brilliance.

The moonlight led her to a basin nestled in one of the temple's many recesses. From this miniature, trickling spring the beam bounced to a sculpted vase eternally pouring water into a basin. Medusa followed the thread of light to a third pool, only to see the light bounce to yet another shining water source across a marble chamber, where it bounced and danced again, and again.

The gleaming, shimmering sliver lured Medusa through the great hall, skipping by sculptures and skirting along the marble floors leading her out onto high steps at the back of the temple.

Medusa looked out over the vast labyrinthine gardens. The moon shone crisp and vibrant in the sky, illuminating the night's moisture upon the statues and flora. The gardens sparkled brilliantly and Medusa could only marvel at the magnificence. She had played in these gardens many times—it was one of her favorite places—but she had never seen it in such splendor.

A deep voice pulled her from her reverie. "Medusa." The call came from behind her and a warm breath on her ear sent shivers down her spine.

She turned, to find nothing, to her amazement, not even the temple. In its place stood a luminous marble wall covered in ivy. She placed her hands upon the stones in disbelief. Had she somehow gotten turned around in her own home? Medusa spun, her mind scrambling for an explanation aside from madness. Could staring into the eclipse have truly addled her mind? Medusa turned again to look out over the garden, but instead found herself standing *in* the garden. She stood deep in lush growth and foliage she had never before seen. It was a place of high ivy hedges and blankets of flora spreading as far as her eyes could see. Delighted by these surroundings, Medusa took in the moonlit splendor, breathing in the crisp air and running her fingertips along the hedges at her hips.

Suddenly, the deep green gave way to well-sculpted marble. Medusa gasped: not ten feet away sat a magnificent fountain, gleaming and shimmering before her. She had never seen this fountain on the grounds. Was she even on temple grounds anymore? Her mind reeled as she walked around the lip of the fountain.

Something about its churning waters reminded Medusa of her forbidden glimpse into the face of the moon. Water in the upper bowls flowed and spilled over finely-fluted white marble into the greater basins below, moving in cascades of liquid silver. Intricate swirls and waves danced with a life of their own—trickling forever over and down.

Hesitantly, Medusa gazed into the fountain's pool. The surface of the water was mirrored glass as she stared down at her own unwavering reflection. Next to her image floated the moon, a perfect miniature replica. She gazed on in wonder, feeling as though she were somehow looking *down* into the night sky. It looked so real, Medusa was compelled to touch the moon's reflection. As she reached, the reflected stars seemed to shift and move, making way for her hand. She touched the surface of the small moon, and in an instant, it was gone—fractured into tiny ripples which swam away.

Medusa leaned back, laughing at herself. Had she actually thought to touch the moon? What a silly girl she must be; she had nearly forgotten she was looking at a mere reflection. Still, she could not help the sadness she felt. The vision had been such a lovely one.

She watched at the fountain's edge, waiting as the moonlit ripples returned, desperately hoping to see the beautiful vision once more. After a few minutes, the water settled and the surface was a mirror once again. However, instead of the brilliant moon, she found her gaze locked on the stunningly bright blue eyes of a handsome young man.

Medusa flew from the side of the fountain, frantically looking at the garden around her. She was met with nothing more than lush greenery. Once she was thoroughly convinced she was alone, Medusa returned to the fountain, breathing deeply to calm her fluttering heart. There, she glanced back into the pool. Nothing. No reflection. No man. No magnificent moon. Just the pale, hazy image of the night sky. Medusa took a long, steadying breath, shook her head, and slowly rose to her feet. She paused, taking one more moment to enjoy the splendor of the hidden garden surrounding her before heading back to her room.

That is, if she could find her room.

What a strange evening. Perhaps this was some illusion, a mysterious dream caused by the eclipse. But if it was, how would she ever wake? Though, she wasn't entirely sure she wanted to wake from this vision.

Smiling sadly to herself, she turned to search for the staircase leading up to the temple, but was stopped by a presence before her. Medusa looked up and there stood a man. Startled, she nearly jumped into the fountain. Catching herself on its marble edge, she looked back up to discover an impossibly tall man. He made no move toward her, but she hurried to the opposite side of the fountain all the same, keeping its rippling waters between them, ready to take flight if the need arose.

The man stood almost as tall as the garden statues and looked to be just as strong. His hair fell in light waves to his shoulders and his eyes were the brightest blue she had ever seen. They practically glowed against the moonlight. He was her age, perhaps a little older, with well-defined shoulders left bare by his blue-silver tunic. The line of his jaw was firm and strong—he possessed the most graceful and attractive face she had ever seen. Medusa's cheeks flushed—she had never thought so well of a man before. As a priestess of Athena, she was not allowed to be in such close proximity to men. She really only ever saw them while gathering alms in the city.

"I am sorry. I did not mean to frighten you," he apologized, his voice direct and calm, and completely soothing. It was liquid silk, and though familiar, she knew she had never heard anything quite like it. It made her think of clear waters flowing over smooth stones.

Medusa struggled to find her voice. When it finally came, her words sprang out like coiled metal, "Who are you?!"

"Pardon my intrusion." His smile came as easily as waves upon the shore and his teeth were pure as white sand.

"Who—why are you here?" she stuttered in confusion.

"I saw you at the festival and had to meet you." His smile was pure charm. "I thought you a muse, come to bring inspiration to this beautiful island. Yet, here I see, you are mortal."

Medusa gaped. "Men are not allowed within these walls so late at night," was all she could think to reply.

"Do you wish me to leave?"

Unsure what she wished, Medusa stood unmoving. She had never been alone with a man. She had been warned of their beguiling ways her entire life. And yet this man seemed to mean her no harm. He appeared soothing and wondrous. Whatever he was, Medusa could not ignore the strange curiosity uncoiling within her.

"Yes," she managed unconvincingly.

"Then I will go."

His words ignited a small pain within her. She did not wish him to leave, but decided to remain silent. He turned away and Medusa's heart sank.

Abruptly the man stopped, as though he could feel her wishing him to stay. "Before I go," he called, turning back, "May I ask of you one thing?"

"You may," she replied with false confidence.

The man smiled broadly this time. It was a smile she somehow recognized. "How is it that a woman as beautiful and talented as you is bound to such a subservient existence?"

She could not hide her surprise as her cheeks flared pink. "You flatter me, sir."

"I have looked upon you from time to time in your years here," he continued. "Every year I am astonished. You have only grown more beautiful, more exquisite. You take my breath away and I wish to know how." His voice had dropped to something more than a whisper.

Medusa's cheeks turned scarlet. She had been complimented before, but it had never set her pulse to fluttering so. "I am but a girl. Surely you exaggerate."

"Might I ask you one more thing?"

Medusa smiled a little at his candor. "Ask," she replied, still maintaining a healthy distance between them.

"Would you sing for me?"

"Sing?" she asked in surprise.

"I have only heard your beautiful voice from afar," he coerced her. "It is so lovely. Might I sample it up close? Just this once? Then, if you still wish, you shall be rid of my presence."

"I cannot sing at this time of night. I might wake one of the sisters."

"No one can hear us here. What better time to sing than under a full moon?"

Medusa considered. What harm would come from singing for the young man? He seemed to have good intentions. "You will leave then?" she asked. "No more questions?"

"Yes. If you wish."

Medusa smiled; he was too polite and cordial to be a danger. "What shall I sing?"

"I believe I once heard a song of a young nymph and her flirtations with a fountain. It would seem fitting here," he replied, gesturing to the elaborate fountain.

"*Love of the Water Nymph*?" she asked.

"Is that the one?" he asked playfully. "Well, it is so lovely."

"I am not sure this is proper...that song is only sung on the *Night of the Goddess*," Medusa whispered hesitantly.

"Ahh, yes. That must have been where I heard it. Beautiful melody. Though not as beautiful as you. It *is* still the night of the festival. Please, indulge me." He moved around to her side of the fountain and sat on its ledge.

Though unnerved by his proximity, she did not move away.

Once settled, he motioned for her to sit next to him. Medusa blushed again and smiled shyly. The handsome stranger had persuaded her.

"It *is* a lovely song." She smiled. "I will sing it for you. Though I confess, I have never sung it by myself before."

"All the better, for yours is the most beautiful voice."

Medusa flushed. "Thank you, sir."

"Please, do not allow me to distract you. Sing. Fill the air with beauty."

Medusa's lips curled into a smile. The man held out his hand and she hesitantly accepted. Luminous in the light of the moon, he sat in content silence, as Medusa's voice—sweet as harps' chords—rang out through the dewy night. As she sang, Medusa's gaze fell to the fountain pond where, to her surprise, she found the very same water nymph of which she sang. Medusa became lost in the song as she watched the beautiful nymph prance upon the mirrored waters.

The nymph was dancing gracefully about the water, when she stopped, having caught a glimpse of her own reflection. Thinking her reflection a partner, she began to dance anew as Medusa's voice unraveled the melody. The nymph pranced and pirouetted, becoming so excited she touched the water's surface. Her reflected dance partner shattered into hundreds of racing ripples. Sad and disappointed, the nymph retreated to the fountain's edge and wept.

Unbeknownst to the nymph, she had an audience. A god looked down upon the sweet, sad creature, and had become so enamored of the nymph's dancing he decided to appear to her, emerging from the fountain as a water sprite. The sad little nymph looked up in surprise, smiled merrily, and with a twirl, began dancing with the cleverly disguised god. There they danced together joyfully on the pool's mirrored surface.

Medusa sang the final chords of the song as the scene slowly faded away. She turned to find herself in the arms of the young man, mid-dance. She hadn't even noticed they had left their seats at the fountain's edge. She had never danced with a man. He was warm and strong, yet the pressure of his arm around her waist was slight and delicate. He was unlike any man she had ever seen.

Medusa felt frightened and yet strangely secure as he leaned in close to her, his lips inches from hers. His soft breath fell upon her cheek and she looked down to hide her blush. However, in looking down, she found the garden was now far below them. Medusa and her dance partner hung in the air, far above the twisting gardens of the Temple! Medusa's grip on the man's shoulders grew tight.

"Don't be afraid," he whispered to her, lightly brushing his lips against her ear as he spoke. His soft words inspired a strange exhilaration within her, as though he could breathe away her worries.

She could feel the heat of the stars reeling past them

as he wrapped his arms firmly around her. His hand gently stroked her hair and he pressed his lips to hers. Medusa's body was afire with a myriad of unknown feelings. Her breath came faster and she hoped beyond all hope the moment would never end.

He gently pulled away, gazing down at her with a smile. Medusa opened her eyes to find she was not flying at all, but standing on the ground at the fountain's edge, in the arms of the tall stranger. She blushed yet again as she pulled away.

"What is wrong?" he asked softly.

"What just happened?" Medusa asked, gazing at the garden in a daze.

"Love," he replied. "Is that such an unknown concept to a priestess of the goddess of wisdom?"

"I know of it," she replied with worry. "But I am to stay…" The words stuck in her throat. "*Untouched*—until I become high priestess."

His lips curled into the slightest hint of a smile. "Do not fret. You have done nothing wrong, broken no vows. It was but a kiss."

Medusa smiled sadly. "You seem to be a nice man, but I think—I think you should go now," she insisted, shocked by her own words.

He stood—disappointment and understanding written on his face. "I will go, but be assured…I will return. The next full moon, if you wish it. We will meet here."

Medusa looked to the ground. If she were caught with a man, she would be disgraced and banished from the temple. However, the thought of turning him away forever was impossibly painful.

When Medusa raised her head to respond, he was gone. She looked everywhere but he was nowhere to be seen. She closed her eyes and took a deep breath.

As she opened her eyes to search for the temple stairs, she found herself not in the garden, but lying in her bed. She bolted upright and stared around the room in disbelief. Could it have been a dream?

A faint glimmering caught her eye. There, on her bedside table lay an elegant silver medallion enveloped in moonlight streaming in from the window. Medusa pulled the necklace closer: on one side was engraved a fountain, on the other a curling wave.

The next morning Medusa woke to larks singing outside her window. She sat up and stretched — memories of the night before slowly flooding her mind. She searched the bedside table, but the silvery amulet was gone. It must have been a dream after all.

Medusa stretched a little more, rubbed the sleep from her eyes, and reluctantly went to her armoire to ready for her daily duties. Gazing into the mirror as she brushed her long golden hair, she caught a glint of light peeking from beneath her robe. Stunned, Medusa moved the robe aside and there, to her amazement and delight, was the amulet, its tiny engraved fountain reflected before her. She smiled brightly. The events of the night before *had* been real. She would see her handsome young man again.

Medusa tucked the amulet back into her robes and

continued about her day, lost in dreams.

On the night of the next full moon, Medusa waited anxiously for the other priestesses to retire. Once the temple was dark, she snuck out to the gardens. Try as she might, she could not find the mysterious fountain. Disappointed, Medusa returned to her chambers, awaiting her handsome stranger. Her heart fluttered as she thought of their last encounter. So many questions reeled through her mind. She fidgeted with the silver medallion as the night wore on. What if he had forgotten her? Full of hope and worry, she tried to stay awake, eager for a sign. However, despite her best efforts, her eyelids fell heavy with sleep.

She was immediately awakened by his voice. Medusa leapt from her bed in search of the silvery moon beam which had guided her at the last full moon. Finding it, she happily followed its glinting light through the hallways and out to the luminous gardens.

Her steps led her directly to the edge of the beautifully engraved fountain. Elated, she sat and ran her hand playfully through the waters, impatient for him to appear. Medusa's heart calmed, her breathing finally slowed, and suddenly he was there, smiling down at her as she sat on the cool marble rim of the fountain.

The two spent the evening at the fountain's edge, wrapped in each other's embrace while she sang.

~~~~

The fog cleared from the crystal's surface as the brittle husk of the lily blew away, circling into the air and disappearing before the darkened crystal eye.

"An enticing tale, Brother," Angus announced, first to break the silence. "Well told."

"I've been holding on to that one for some time." Killian nodded. "It is a long tale to tell."

"I look forward to hearing more."

"In good time," Killian replied.

Angus sighed, a slightly exasperated strain in his breath. "I believe I hear Banon on his way down. I'm sure his offerings will be interesting……to say the least."

The door to the room opened without so much as a courtesy knock and Banon strutted in. His darkly tanned skin made his Cheshire smile stand out all the more; the light caramel-brown of his eyes was nearly as bright as his sun-bleached dreads. His clothing was in the fashion of the sailors in days long gone: a weathered, high-collared leather coat and billowing undershirt. He seemed to have just stepped off the rolling decks of a tall ship.

"Hello, my brothers. I have come with a plethora of offerings," he said merrily, taking a seat at the great table.

"You are late, Banon," Angus scolded.

"Do you have any idea what traffic is like from the Playa Del Rey docks? It's murder, even at this hour. I see you all started without me, though."

"Your clothing is not entirely appropriate for this

land. Did you not think to change into something more suitable for the time?"

"And make myself even more tardy? Besides, I do not believe the people of this world truly care about such things. On the way here, I passed a group that looked straight out of a medieval circus."

"He has a point," Killian defended. "The fashion of this world has become too muddled for even its people to keep up. I am sure he brought finer clothing for tomorrow's ball."

"Finest clothes a man can steal." Banon smiled.

Angus nodded but it was clear he did not care for his younger brother's brazen nature. "Have you seen Conner?"

"He is no doubt distracted by the many electric wonders of this land. You know how he is."

"How fare your shipmates?" Patrick asked, changing topic.

"They're as well as they can be… considering *you-know-who*."

"He is not so bad," Killian defended.

"Yeah," Banon scoffed. "I bet he's a real peach when you don't work for him."

"So, you have many offerings?" Patrick interjected.

"I do. Tidings of a new crewmate," Banon replied, riffling through his pockets. "Well, as new as a crewman can be aboard an immortal pirating ship."

"Sounds interesting. Origin stories are always a favorite of the Fates."

"I'll get on with it then," he replied, bowing his head to the dark eye. When he looked up again his gold eyes quickly misted over. "I offer this tale of a young man who joined a crew he was not prepared to meet—but needed more than he knew. A brave young fellow who escaped his dreary life and cast his fortune upon the wind. I present this old compass, once passed through his hands."

With that, Banon placed a sea-worn wood and metal compass upon the oak stump table. The brothers bowed their heads as the compass began spinning in place.

MARITIME

The shadowy sails of a ship were just visible on the horizon. Jonathan Maritime sighed in relief; days had passed and not once had he seen another craft. Not so much as a fishing boat had drifted by — hell, not so much as a fish.

The crew of the *Scurvy Wretch* had managed well enough on supplies, but they had only set out with a week's worth of rations. *Fourteen* days they had been afloat and they'd just consumed the last of their bread.

This small cargo ship was the first vessel Jonathan had been elected to navigate, and fortune — the finicky minx — refused to smile upon him. A bad wind had come. They had suffered nothing but dull weather, choppy waters, and a malfunctioning rudder.

The situation was made even worse by the captain—a gluttonous sloth of a man who consumed double his rations every night. In a drunken rage over the storm-damaged rudder responsible for setting them off course, the captain had blamed Jonathan and thrown his maps and compass overboard, calling them useless trinkets. Jonathan's skills were such that he could have gotten them home by the stars, but the heavy clouds overhead refused to subside. Even the sun's positioning could not be read thanks to the damnable weather.

Jonathan stared up dismally at the distress flag flapping limply in the lifeless wind. He'd been ready to give up all hope when the dark vessel had appeared in the distance. The oncoming ship appeared to have the trappings of the Royal Armada, same hull style, same mast and rigging. Jonathan almost laughed in relief: help was on the way. It would be the first bit of luck they'd encountered thus far.

He squinted at the oncoming ship through the quickly diminishing light, dreaming of a cozy bed back at port; however, as their rescuers came closer, his hope died with the lowering of its Royal Armada flag. In its place now flew a flag with black swords crossed against a white background.

Pirates.

Jonathan ran below to the captain who lolled about in a rum-addled daze. He warned the mate and other crew members of the coming threat, but they paid him no mind. Panicked, he hurried to the bell and rang it, calling all men to arms. The captain, snapped out of his coma by the alarm bell, stormed onto the deck after him.

"What's all this?" the captain hollered, hauling Jonathan away from the bell by his shirt collar.

Jonathan merely pointed to the grappling hooks flying from the enemy boat onto their own decks. The crew set to cutting the ropes tethering their dead ship to the attacking vessel, but it was no use. The *Scurvy Wretch* was quickly overrun.

Shots rang out and steel clashed as the crew attempted to fight off the raiders. The *Scurvy Wretch*'s men numbered only fifteen, most of them malcontent sailors, but there were a few worth their salt. Regardless, they were no match for the skilled miscreants of the great dark ship.

The battle was short-lived, and Jonathan quickly found himself kneeling with a sword point pressing into his back. He was disgusted to think he would end his days upon this wretched boat. Even in starvation there had been hope of a favorable wind to blow them back to shore, but now, even that small hope was naught but a fading memory.

Jonathan watched as a great plank slammed onto the railing of the *Wretch*, spanning the gap between the two. More pirates strolled onto deck, searching every corner for valuables.

"Who's in charge here?" a wiry blond man demanded. All turned to the captain, who swayed drunkenly on his knees. "You're joking. No wonder you're out to drift. This man couldn't captain a dinghy."

"Knox, don't play with the captives," came a strong voice. The voice had a strange resonance to it, somewhat scratchy, but not the usual baritone of a man at sea.

"Yes, Captain," the blond replied, straightening up and quickly directing a few men to check the cargo hold.

Jonathan kept his head low hoping to encourage the scum to leave him his life. Then his shipmates froze. They knelt, staring straight ahead with jaws agape. Confused, he followed their gaze to a tall figure wearing a red sash and a wide-brimmed hat, a scarlet feather waving from its band. Slim and sharp as a dagger, the figure was topped by a massive tangle of auburn hair that flowed in the wind. The captain of the invading ship cut the oddest figure Jonathan had ever seen on water. The realization slowly dawned on him: the figure was no *man*. Only once had Jonathan seen a woman don clothing in this manner, but the memory was a painful one on which he did not want to dwell.

"Since your captain is...indisposed, I wish someone to explain your plight," the lady announced.

"I answer to no woman," called a surly old snaggletooth.

"As you wish." Her voice indifferent. "String him up." In an instant snaggletooth was trussed and carried away.

The woman looked to the next man, who only sneered. "I suppose you have a similar answer for me."

The man would not speak, but quickly found his voice when her crewman pulled him out of line and stuffed him—headfirst—into an empty barrel. Panicked screams split the air and Jonathan turned in time to see snaggletooth fall from the crow's nest. He cringed, waiting to hear the crunching of bones on the deck. Instead, there was a loud *twang* as a rope around snaggletooth's leg went taught, a mere foot before his face connected with the deck.

Cheering sounded in the crow's nest. "Look, Captain!" one of the men shouted. "I finally got the rope right!"

The captain did not smile. She simply motioned for them to return, and looked back to the man next to Jonathan, waiting for a reply.

"Ship don't move," the man told her shakily. He was a simpleton who could hardly form sentences, but he was proud, so proud that Jonathan knew he too would end up dangling from his boot straps were he to continue speaking.

"The rudder was damaged in the storm," Jonathan called, hoping to save the stubborn man from sharing the fates of snaggletooth and the silent man.

The fearsome woman turned, looking at him for the first time. She would have been a beauty, if not for the thin scar running the length of her face.

"You will speak for the ship then," she announced, and the man holding Jonathan hauled him to his feet before her. The woman's eyes were impossibly green—and familiar.

"There is no wind, the rudder is broken, and we

have no compass or map."

"Seems you are having a run of bad luck." She gave a slight nod and three of her men scrambled to verify the truth of Jonathan's claims.

"As I said, the ship was damaged in the storm," Jonathan continued. "We have been afloat for days and have no food. I am just the navigator. Take what you want, but please let it not come to bloodshed."

The woman glared at him as her men returned to confirm the status of the ship. She nodded to them in dismissal. "You carry weapons and medicine," the woman told Jonathan. "Cure and cause in one shipment."

"Bit ironic, isn't it." Jonathan laughed nervously.

There was something in her eye he recognized. For a second it seemed she recognized him too, but she turned before he could be sure.

"Take the weapons. Leave the medicine," she commanded to his surprise and her men quickly carried a dozen crates onto their ship. "Your rudder will be mended, roughly. It will hold until you make port. The weather should clear soon," she told Jonathan and headed back to the railing, and her ship.

"Do you need a navigator?" He had no idea where the question sprang from, it was an inexplicable outburst, but the thought of going back to port with the pitiful crew of the *Wretch* was too pathetic.

"You wish to lead us into a storm as well?" she asked coldly.

Jonathan hung his head in shame as she continued up the plank.

Her men followed until only Knox remained. "Come on, then," the blond man called to Jonathan. "Captain McBane doesn't like to be kept waiting."

In a flash, Jonathan was on his feet and hurrying toward the plank where Knox handed him a spare compass and nodded at the slovenly captain of the *Scurvy Wretch*.

Jonathan checked the instrument and tossed it to the lush. "Port is northwest," he told the wretched man and headed across the gangplank to the massive hull of the sinister ship.

The great dark vessel took off like a shot and Jonathan with it. Turned out the bad winds were merely those of change.

~~~~

"Not bad, no?" Banon beamed at his brothers, as what was left of the old compass flaked away in tiny wood and metal chips.

"It's not a competition, Banon," Angus replied. "Yours is a simple story, yet well told. It's been accepted.

"Don't worry; I have plenty more where that came from."

"I hold my breath in anticipation," Angus scoffed and turned to his brothers. "Now that you've shared, I suppose it's my turn."

"Since you apparently think you can do better," Banon muttered.

"Go on, Brother," Patrick encouraged Angus. "Give

your offering."

Angus pulled an ancient coin from his pocket and placed it upon the table. This simple gesture was all the brothers needed to look to the heart of the table yet again. Angus's eyes clouded.

"I offer this ancient story of a being who has seen much in his infinite life. This coin—possessing his likeness—was printed at the height of his power. This tale is his account of both his origin and his fall."

The ancient coin began to tarnish and wear, losing contour and definition—as though passing through countless hands over many, many centuries.

REMY

My name is Remy Martin—yes, like the Cognac. However, this is not my given name. Once, long before America was discovered, my name was Romulus of Rome. It is strange to be over two thousand years old and have the love of my life compare me to "a lot of broken statues and gladiators." I try to remind her that they were new when I was born but my love only laughs and returns to her video games. That is how it is in this day and age, so quick to forget the past.

I only wish I could forget it so easily. I have many times witnessed first bloodshed in war—I have been a silent spectator to the rise and fall of nearly every great civilization in the world.

There have been many different tellings of my tale, with many different versions. But this one is mine. When I was known as Romulus, my Brother Remus and I founded the city of Rome. Our origin is complicated: filled with treachery, abandonment, victory, and revenge. With the blood of the god Mars coursing in our veins and the temperaments of wolves, no one could defeat us. No one, that is, but ourselves, thus this tale is not of my birth, but of my death.

Once my brother and I built the magnificent city of Rome, I was elected King. Unfortunately, my brother was not pleased with the decision. He became distant and reclusive. Remus spent his time building a wall around the city, claiming we needed fortification. Though the city was under no threat, he insisted on exerting endless hours and resources to his folly.

Upon completion of his gods-forsaken wall, I challenged his claims that no man could penetrate his barrier and survive. To my utter chagrin, my brother chose to prove the wall's effectiveness himself. As I and my court looked on, a newly determined Remus vaulted over the wall; however, before he could set foot on the other side, the god Pluto claimed him. Pluto took him as sacrifice so that no army could overtake our city's wall.

Remus and I had overcome so many odds we thought ourselves immortal. Rumors even circulated that I had somehow murdered my brother. We had the strength and speed of the gods, but as we came to learn, we lacked the gods' everlasting ability to live.

I was left to rule the empire alone, feeling the weight of my brother's death profoundly. A short time later, I formed a group of several men who would act as leaders to my regions and help me rule. However, I knew that one day I too would die. Though the men I had chosen to stand beside were good men, they could be lead astray by viperous men wishing to take their power.

I could not have that.

In fear of my brother's fate and the impending shuffling off of my own mortal coil, I set out to find the Gates of Tartarus, the very opening to the fearsome underworld. I intended to take up the matter with Pluto himself and secure my own immortality. Without my leadership, Rome would perish.

It took me years to find Pluto. When I did, he turned out to be one of the more reasonable gods. I had expected a fight. Instead, he advised me to live my life and abandon my search for immortality. I have wished many a night I had heeded his words. When Pluto realized I would not be swayed, he grudgingly suggested I pay a visit to Lilith, but to be wary of any gifts she may bestow upon me.

High in the mountains over Rome I found her, living alone in a lavish villa overlooking my metropolis. Lilith had a veil of long blond hair, cunning blue eyes, and a beauty beyond compare. How such a woman so close to my domain had escaped my attention, I did not know. When I asked for the secret of her immortality, she revealed to me an eternity of nights feeding off the life's blood of my people.

I had returned home to rule, immortality in hand, but the price I paid to claim it was dear. No longer could I see my beautiful city by the light of day. My hunger, ever present drove me to feed on those closest to me. Lilith had warned me not to let myself get hungry, lest I attack the closest source of blood. I had not listened.

One particularly terrible night, I had tempted to hide myself away from my council. I was rabid with hunger and therefore locked myself in my study. I would be able to contain myself there, no one else could get in save for the general of my army and my trusted advisor, Maximus—the one other person who had the key to my study. Several of my advisors had come and gone attempting to draw me from the room, but I would not unlatch the door.

Late that night, at the height of my hungered craze, I remember hearing the door unlatch. I tried to yell a warning but all that came out was a growl. I looked up and saw General Maximus standing in the door. Against my will, I attacked. Before I was overcome by bloodlust, I saw a feminine shadow lingering in the hallway. It was Lilith—she had led the general to me.

I will forever mourn General Maximus, the leader of Rome's greatest army. He was the closest thing I'd had to a friend since my brother. He deserved a better death.

I was reluctant to accustom myself to such a life of horror and regret. Alas, I was helpless before Lilith's beguiling beauty and sinister charm; she held a power over me I could not fight. In seeking her, I had traded my freedom for immortality.

I had wanted to live forever, but not like this.

I continued to rule over Rome for many decades, but as Lilith's influence over me grew, so did her influence over Rome. Under her power, Rome transformed into a brutal, cutthroat society determined to conquer every land within its reach by any means necessary. She was power-hungry: demanding sanguine tribute from the people. When I did not concede, she would descend upon the city and force me to help her bloody my fair streets.

When my maker was not appeased, crimson cries of the proletariat and aristocracy alike echoed through the alleys. She orchestrated wars and drove me to dominate neighboring countries through terrible and atrocious means. The night we took Sabine was horrifying, one which will remain forever etched in my memory. The screams of the men and women haunt me to this day.

Rome could not survive in this manner. Crops dwindled along with the people. Mobs formed. A civil war loomed on the horizon and I would not, could not, allow my beloved Rome to be torn asunder by her own citizenry. I made a desperate decision: one night, in the midst of a terrible thunderstorm, I left Rome.

I slipped from Lilith near dawn and began my long journey, hiding in caves during the day and traveling by night. When I could not find humans on which I might feed, I lived off what animals were near. Each moment was torment as I felt her calling, beckoning me to return.

I sought Pluto, begging to be released from my bond with Lilith. Unfortunately, I was beyond even his help.

My only remaining option, Pluto asserted, was to kill her; but in doing so, I would damage myself terribly. Our blood-bond was all encompassing; I would live, but my soul would be torn asunder. Pluto assured me I would one day heal, but not before passing through *centuries* of loneliness, anger, and desolation. I knew I would rather live an eternity in pain than continue to be enslaved by Lilith.

I made the long journey back to Rome with the secret to Lilith's demise. Her wrath was terrible. As punishment, Lilith locked me away until my own hunger drove me mad. She then loosed me on my own army: I demolished an entire battalion before coming to my senses. I was sickened as I looked upon the horror I had wrought upon the people of Rome—*my* people. I had become a bane to the very home I had created, to the very city I sought to protect.

Lilith had to be stopped.

With loathing, I acted as Lilith's obedient slave until she was confident in the totality of my submission to her every whim. It was a long year of unspeakable torment to me, but my people were safe from her horrors, and would soon be forever.

One morning while she slept, I forced myself

awake, and snuck into her chambers. There, I cut off her head, burned the body, and carried her ashes to the temple of Pluto where I asked for his acceptance of her infernal remains. As her ashes flew up onto the winds, I knew Pluto had heeded my pleas: Lilith was gone. In that moment I crumpled, feeling as though the heart had been ripped from my chest. It was torture beyond anything I had ever experienced. Yet, I was free from her control—I was a free Roman once again. I would have rid the world of her presence a hundred times over, regardless of this wrenching in my chest.

Once I was able, I returned home. There, I vowed never to make another of my kind. Unfortunately, when I reached the city of Rome I found her so changed she was no longer mine. However, knowing she was safe from Lilith, I decided it was time to go my own way.

I ceased to be Romulus of Rome. From then on, I had no name. I wandered the world a shred of my former self, in pain and utter devastation. True to Pluto's word, my torment lasted *centuries*.

Then, one day, when I felt as though I had nearly become accustomed to my suffering, the pain subsided and I began to heal. With no goal for the long life ahead of me, I settled in Europe in a land called *Britain*, before it acquired the *Great*. It had once been part of my own territories, making it familiar enough to be a comfort and yet different enough that I could exist without constant reminders of my past.

From Britain, I moved to France and settled near a small commune: Point-Remy. I spent many years in this idyllic locale. As the people came to know me, they bestowed upon me the name of their patron saint — Saint Remigius — and affectionately referred to me as *Remy*. The people and their saint reminded me of the home I once knew in Rome, before the death of my brother, where life was divine and we were loved by our people. I spent nearly a century in Point-Remy, and though I loved my home in France, I eventually had to leave.

I changed cities every few decades, continents on occasion. I even fought in wars when necessary. Mars still favored me in battle and I won every skirmish in which I participated. When I eventually tired of the world and its politics, I settled in the New Americas to sit back and watch the human play unfold around me. There, I adopted the last name of Martin after the distiller of my favorite Cognac, and Remy Martin was born.

Slowly but surely, supernatural beings settled in this new Land of Opportunity and wreaked much havoc, particularly throughout the American South. I helped the supernatural law, the Order, establish rules to keep more fearsome and stubborn supernaturals in line. The Order eventually discovered my history and began referring to me by my given name.

Romulus existed once again.

This time as enforcer instead of king. My former name drives terror into the minds of those who are familiar with my terrible deeds. However, to myself, I remain Remy Martin: a solitary immortal who becomes Romulus only when needed.

In all this time, I had kept my vow never to make another. That was, until Pluto—who is more popularly known now by the name Hades, or simply Death—called upon me for a favor. I have tried to relay this story to my love, but as such a young creature she, unfortunately, has the attention span of a gnat. One day she may listen and she may become frightened of my past. But ultimately, it makes little difference. We are who we are—we are bound to one another, and not even time can sever these bonds.

~~~~

The brothers were riveted to the dark crystal, their eyes aglow. Having finished his tale, Angus's eyes began to clear. However, instead of turning their normal golden brown, his irises went black.

Strange images danced on the surface of the dense crystal eye. Brief indistinct visions of a dark creature. Then the form abruptly cleared, as did the blackened film from Angus's eyes, leaving the brothers in a startled daze. Blinking heavily, they looked to one another in confusion.

Killian cleared his throat and ran a hand through his short grecian mane. "Based on that reaction, I would say the conclusion to your story was rejected, Brother."

"No, not rejected," Angus replied. "I would think you'd recognize a *warning* when you saw one, Killian."

"A warning?" Banon asked, his short blond dreadlocks hanging in his face.

"Something is on its way. The Eye rarely acts on its

own. But—"

"But?" Patrick's voice was tense.

"But," Angus continued, "It did act of its own accord a few days ago. I'm sure it's the Fates."

"And you think they're trying to tell us something?" Patrick asked.

"Whatever it is, I think I know what's being said…"

"The Titans?" Banon asked, uncharacteristically stern.

"Yes." Angus looked out at his brothers through his deep curtain of long dark dreadlocks. "It would explain the disturbances."

"What do we do?" Patrick asked, looking from one brother to another.

"Nothing."

"You can't be serious!" Killian's palm came down upon the table, startling them all.

"There's not enough to interpret," Angus calmly replied. "What can we do against the unknown? All we can do is be at our best and prepare for the worst. I suggest we all get a grip." He looked pointedly at Killian, then at Patrick. "Let us continue the offerings."

"He's right," Killian replied. "It is the source of our being. We must go on."

"Agreed," Patrick seconded.

"Let us continue then," Angus sighed. "Banon, why don't you offer another?"

"Gladly," Banon replied, still slightly rattled. "I offer another tale of the Navigator's travels. A tale in which he battles to earn his place amongst his new brethren." Banon held a small translucent bottle containing several bristly hairs so thick they almost appeared spike-like. "I bring the hairs of a deceitful sea creature whose trickery nearly cost the crew their ship."

Uncorking the bottle, he let the hairs slip from the glass onto the great oak table where they proceeded to pop and sear. The brothers bowed their heads.

THE STORM

As amused as Jonathan was by his new crewmates, being kicked awake every morning had grown tiresome. He was weary of fighting his way to a wash station filled with greasy remnants of the crew, then trudging his way into a galley to find hardly a scoop of gruel to start the day.

The crew had developed a habit of picking on Jonathan. They placed squid in his bunk, fish in his ditty bag, and urchin in his clothing. Reaching the deck every morning, the first thing thrust upon him was a mop and bucket. Though he knew he needed to earn the crew's respect, being forced to swab the deck when he should be plotting the course for the day was infuriating at best.

"Maritime, aft cabin on the double!" Knox yelled down into the galley.

Jonathan sat stunned a moment. It had been days since he had heard the first mate call for him.

Since boarding the *Persephone*, Jonathan had only seen Captain McBane a handful of times. The woman kept to herself, communing mainly with Knox, her first mate. Knox seemed to be a good man but was lax in punishing crew shenanigans. The men were sure to never abuse Jonathan outright, but unfortunately, Knox was not always around.

The worst of all the crew was their boatswain— Lido. He was a small man determined to make up for his lack of stature with an abundance of bad attitude. Lido was in charge of delegating Knox's orders, and often changed those orders to benefit himself. Nothing Jonathan ever did was good enough for the unpleasant little man. The deck was never clean enough; the ropes never coiled properly, the bosun's locker never organized correctly. Jonathan prided himself on a reasonably meticulous nature—one had to be precise and organized when plotting routes—but even he could not live up to Lido's standards.

Happy to have some actual navigating to do in the aft, Jonathan stopped peeling potatoes and headed for the deck.

Jonathan might have been able to handle all of this mistreatment were he still permitted to navigate. However, every time Knox called for help in plotting their course, Lido made sure Jonathan had some other matter to attend. Jonathan rarely saw the quarter deck, let alone the aft cabin where he was to check the ship logs and chart their course. Jonathan was a slight fellow and not good for much physically—but on a starless night he could find his way, figure the direction of the wind in the slightest breeze, and sense a storm from miles away. He was made to be a navigator, not a deckhand. Jonathan tried to bring the matter to Knox's attention, but getting the spirited first mate to slow down enough to listen proved fruitless.

Perhaps Knox would have an open ear this time.

As annoying as Lido was, life on the *Persephone* was still far better than his life aboard the *Scurvy Wretch*. This crew lacked for nothing and almost always had a favorable wind. In all honesty, Jonathan's navigation skills would not have been much needed even if he were allowed to step away from his menial chores.

It was then he heard the distant booming of a dreaded thunder. It was faint, had he not a trained ear, he might not have noticed. By the sounds of it, they were heading straight for a storm.

Jonathan was halfway to the deck when Lido's boots appeared in front of him.

"Where d'ya think you're going?" Lido yelled down at Jonathan.

"Knox called for me. There's a storm coming. I need to check the charts."

"What storm? I didn't hear anything from Knox. His orders go through me," the little man insisted. "Navigator or no, you aren't getting out of spud duty."

"No offense, sir, but we're headed south. I heard the thunder. We're on course with a bad storm. It'll be on us by dusk. We need to redirect the ship."

"Do you want the crew to starve?"

Jonathan knew this argument would get him nowhere. "No, sir. Please, just tell Knox four knots east should steer us away."

"If there's even a storm," he scoffed. "Finish up and I'll think about telling him."

"Thank you, sir."

With that, Jonathan headed back into the galley. He was sure Knox could handle the situation, but Jonathan could not quell the uneasy feeling in his gut.

The thunder grew louder as the time passed. The *Persephone* had not altered course. The booming in the distance rattled the hull with its force. Fierce streaks of lightning quickly followed. Jonathan scrubbed the Galley floor tensely, he couldn't take this any more. The storm was unavoidably upon them now. Unless they wanted to take an unscheduled trip to Tartarus, he needed to do something.

Jonathan dropped the useless scrubbing Lido had assigned him and quickly headed aft. He got as far as the main deck when Lido caught up with him.

"What'd I tell you?" he hollered. "Get below!"

Jonathan continued past the irate little man and toward the stern. It was useless to argue, the man had no care for reason. Jonathan was nearly to the top of the quarter deck stair when Lido snatched him by the coat collar.

"I'll teach you to listen to me!" he yelled, yanking him down.

Jonathan hit the deck hard and scrambled to his feet. "Don't you see the storm? Are you blind? Can't you hear the thunder, smell it on the wind?!"

Lido stood affronted, it was the first time Jonathan had actually stood up for himself. "I'll have you flogged before the night's out!" he yelled and started toward Jonathan when Knox appeared at the top of the stairs.

"What is going on—" Knox cut himself short at the sight of Jonathan. "There you are, Maritime! The Captain may think you're some brilliant navigator, but you're bloody worthless if you can't be found!"

"Sir?" Jonathan couldn't keep the confusion from his face.

"There is a storm coming, boy! If you haven't noticed we're heading straight for it. I've been trying to steer us out of these currents for the better part of an hour!"

"That's why we haven't turned?"

"Every time I sent for you, Lido reported that you were indisposed! Irresponsible, Maritime!"

Jonathan glared back at Lido. The little pitbull of a man backed away, clearly unprepared to abuse Jonathan in front of Knox. Now would be the perfect time for revenge, but Jonathan refused to waste more time.

"I kept trying to warn you about the storm. It's fierce, I can tell by the thunder," he told Knox as they headed to the aft. "Have you found an alternate course?"

"No. I can read the weather like the back of my hand, but charting has never been my forte. These things read like Sanskrit."

It had been merely raining when Jonathan had last come onto the deck, but the closer they got to the storm, the lower the barometer dropped, turning the rain to hail.

"Please, allow me," he told Knox calmly.

Jonathan pored over the charts, checked the compass, and scanned the ship's log. The *Persephone* was several miles off the nearest coast and heading straight into this beast of a storm. Jonathan saw they'd missed their last chance of escape more than ten nautical miles ago. Digging his fingers into his hair, he kept his head bowed to the charts, convinced he'd find a way out of this tempest. He calculated every angle and route. They had *one* chance: a deep cross current which ran across the *Persephone*'s path just a few short miles away.

If they didn't make that, they would be in serious trouble.

"The gale is miles wide," he told Knox. "The winds alone will tear off our sails. If we turn east, we can catch the cross current out, skirting the thing. It'll be rough waters, but we can get out with our skin. That is, so long as we're not pulled back in."

Knox cast a suspicious look at the instruments.

"This isn't an exact science," Jonathan continued. "A storm like this can create a whirlpool effect that could pull her back in. Even a bad wave could ruin our chances of escape. We have to be careful and we have to act fast."

Knox nodded and hurried to the helm where he announced their heading to the crew and instructed them to attach their lifelines.

Immediately, they went to work.

Knox nearly had the ship on course when the wheel jerked to a stop, the hull and stays creaking in protest. Jonathan hurried to help, taking the other side of the wheel, but even with their combined efforts, it would not turn.

"The currents have the rudder! They're too strong," Knox yelled over the wind.

It was then that Captain McBane ascended the stair to the helm and looked out at the storm. "What is this?" she yelled, as if scolding the skies would stop the hail now pelting her crew. "Knox, report!"

"Just a spot of rough weather, Captain," Knox replied, struggling with the wheel.

"Storm's been on the horizon for hours. Why didn't we sail around?"

"Been trying, Captain. It's massive. Currents have been keeping the boat on course with it."

"Maritime. Have we plotted a new course?"

"I, uh—sort of."

"Sort of?" Her voice was colder than the hail rattling around their feet.

"I haven't been allowed up to the aft cabin for most of the trip, Captain, but I think I might be able to p-pull us out of this," Jonathan stuttered lightly.

"Weren't *allowed* to the aft cabin? Who wouldn't *allow* you?" McBane's voice was steel.

Jonathan looked to Lido, who was now backing down the stair to the main deck. McBane immediately turned to the little man.

"He just joined the ship. He needs to learn his place," Lido explained, continuing backward.

"*Learn his place*? You have been with us nearly as long." Even in the dismal light, Jonathan could see the color flaring in McBane's cheeks. "He is our navigation expert. What, exactly, do you feel he needs to *learn*?"

As Lido stammered his response, an odd bluish glint came to his eye. As the captain glared on, the man before them began to shift and alter. Thinking at first it was a trick of the hail and the wind, it took a moment for the crew to realize what they were seeing: Lido's skin took on a pearly opaqueness as hair sprouted thick and bristly in a spiked helm over his head and down the back of his neck.

The captain's sword was at Lido's neck in an instant. "What are you?" she demanded.

Lido lowered his head, eyes fully blue now, no whites to be seen. "You do not tread in my lord's water. No matter who you sail under." His voice rippled in and out, as though he spoke from underwater. His message delivered, he lunged for the railing and leapt from the deck into the icy waters below.

Jonathan and Knox ran after Lido, but there was no trace of him in the dark roiling depths.

Jonathan stood shocked—not by Lido's sudden leap

but by the way the man's skin had glistened like the sea itself before plunging to his grave.

"What in the name of the god's was that?" Jonathan could not tear his eyes from the edge of the ship.

"The gods being troublesome," McBane replied and ran back up to the helm. "Knox, we've been sabotaged. Man the helm!" she commanded a nearby crewman. "Maritime, are you with us, or do I have to navigate us out of this storm myself?"

Like a shot, Jonathan took off up the stairs, across the quarter deck, and down into the aft cabin after McBane and Knox.

"It appears Lido has been keeping our new navigator from the charts so we would end our days in the thralls of this cursed storm," McBane told Knox. "Let's see if he can keep us from going belly up in this trap."

Quickly, Jonathan scanned the charts. They had not yet missed their last opportunity to avoid the storm. "In two miles we need to tack and head east."

"Tack in two miles?" Knox scoffed. "Are you crazy? She'll capsize."

"No, look at the waters," Jonathan directed. "They are flowing *toward* the storm. We can still turn into the cross current ahead. If we catch the winds at the right moment, we can use our own wake to break the course."

"And if we don't?" Knox asked.

"Well, capsizing is as bad as it gets. Right?"

"One would think," McBane glowered as the wind whipped at the sails, challenging the lines which held them fast.

"There it is!" Jonathan pointed to the churning line of water ahead.

"How could you possibly see that in this weather?" Knox yelled over the storm.

"It's what I do," Jonathan replied. The ship swayed and jerked as hail pummeled the deck, but he stared ahead, barely blinking. "Now!" his shout came at the exact moment their wake met with the cross-flow.

The sails flapped like thundering birds as Knox and McBane cranked the wheel. The ship moaned in protest, but they forced her off the turbulent waters and into the deep current.

The *Persephone* shifted, leaning precariously so the whole crew clutched the railings to keep from sliding into the treacherous depths. As fingers began to slip and feet to scramble on the slick deck, the groaning ship hit her own wake. She shuttered terribly, launching several men overboard. Lines snapped taut as the wind tore sails from their stays, shredding them to tatters. The crew was sure she'd be shaken into driftwood—when suddenly, she righted herself.

The current slowly led them away from the storm and out to calmer seas. Pulling in the lines of their mates thrown overboard, the crew grimaced as more than one severed and frayed rope was pulled back. Those who survived were worse for wear, but still able to pull breath. McBane removed her hat and bowed her head. The crew followed suit and silence encompassed the *Persephone* as her crew grieved.

Slowly the rain ceased, the wind died, and the sun rose above the ominous storm clouds.

"I must thank you for leading us away from the storm in one piece," McBane told Jonathan. "Your new quarters will be in the aft cabin." She turned to her crew. "If I catch anyone keeping crew members from their duties, they will answer to me. Now, thank your navigator for keeping the ship and her wretched crew afloat!"

The men all cheered and Jonathan stood stunned. No one had ever cheered for him.

Once the applause died away, the crew went about repairing the ship and Jonathan found himself swamped with thankful crew mates. Nodding and clasping many clammy, blistered hands, he caught sight of McBane heading to her quarters. He extricated himself from his shipmates and stopped the captain just short of her door.

"I am sorry I could not help in time to save everyone."

"You did a brave thing," she assured him. "The sea takes whom it pleases. They are not the first casualties of the *Persephone* and I dare say they will not be the last."

"Might I ask, what happened with Lido? You seemed unsurprised when he dove into the waters. What did he mean when he said he does not care who we sail under? Who *do* we sail under?"

"The sea is a strange place filled with many anomalies. This will not be the last bizarre sight you see. In time you will learn our purpose, Mr. Maritime. When you do, you may again choose not to sail with us."

Jonathan gaped in surprise. Again? This was the first time she had addressed their previous encounters.

"Until then, go about your duty," she said briskly and disappeared into her quarters.

Jonathan bit back the urge to pester her with more questions; she was the captain—despite their past. He dare not overstep his bounds.

The next morning, he awoke to the sound of the roosters they kept for supper—instead of a boot in his ribs. When he reached the galley, there was a fresh pot of porridge and loaves of bread. In lieu of scorning, his fellow crewmates offered more praise for his heroics of the night before.

When he began his day, the aft cabin was ready and waiting. The cabin boy had laid out his charts and polished his instruments.

Finally, Jonathan Maritime was home.

~~~~

The mist cleared from Banon's eyes as the final shreds of the sea creature's hairs smoked into vapor.

"Your navigator seems a very adaptable creature," Patrick commented.

"He has more strength than even he admits. The man has recently moved on to a...less-hazardous crew, but Jonathan was a great addition to our crew and his tales continue. I have several more."

"Delightful," Patrick replied. "I envy your travels on the sea. You inspire me, Brother. Perhaps I'll take a vacation soon, travel more of the lands."

"Let me know how that goes. I could use a break myself." Banon laughed.

"Who's next?" Angus asked the small group.

"If I may." Killian pulled a small hand, carved from stone, out of his coat pocket. "I offer the downfall of a beautiful and innocent creature. A creature doomed to a desolation reserved for the foulest of transgressors. I present this once-living flesh, turned by the eye of the cursed gorgon herself."

Killian placed the hand upon the table where it began to gray and crack.

MEDUSA'S DOWNFALL

Once again, it came time for the *Night of the Goddess*. The last full moon before the night of the eclipse, as each full moon before it, Medusa awoke and followed the silvery beam to the moonlit fountain. She awaited her beloved, but somehow, this night felt imbalanced. The waters of the fountain never settled, the moonlight was dim, the garden less lush, and a strange chill hung in the air.

Medusa sat at the fountain, immersed in uneasiness. Fretfully, she waited.

Suddenly, strong arms wrapped around her and she leapt away.

"I did not mean to frighten you." His voice was calm and soothing, as always. Medusa flushed with relief and rushed into his arms. "What is the matter?"

"Do you feel it?" she asked warily.

He stopped and went suddenly rigid. Medusa pulled back to look up at him. His demeanor had shifted so suddenly she nearly gasped.

"I missed it," he cursed himself. Medusa could see the worry in his eyes. "She wouldn't dare harm you."

Medusa's heart sank. "She?"

"Athena has followed me." Medusa's eyes grew wide with fear. She always knew her moonlit paramour was not a common mortal, but she never dreamed this would involve her beloved goddess. "I know you are here," he called to the gardens.

There was a shift in the ivy draping the wall opposite the fountain. Medusa could not stifle her gasp as a tall, impossibly beautiful woman stepped out from behind the wall. She was the very same figure immortalized in marble on the central pedestal of the temple's great hall. Medusa's breath caught in her throat as she stared at her patron goddess and quickly shifted her eyes to the garden floor, humbled to look upon her.

"So! This is where you disappear to, Poseidon?" Athena's voice was thick with scorn. "You have been so scarce in Olympus. I should have known you would be trifling in my affairs."

Medusa stared at her beloved in astonishment. She had thought him magical—a muse or a sprite perhaps. But not *the* Poseidon.

Poseidon glared at Athena coldly, keeping Medusa protectively behind him. "I have broken no rules," he told the goddess. "I have not stepped foot in your temple."

"You have my priestess!"

"She is here of her own accord. I have not bewitched her. She has been neither harmed nor sullied."

"This is *my* island. Zeus will have your head when I tell him of your indiscretion." Athena was almost hissing in her anger.

"King of the gods or no, I have no fear of my brother. I have not set foot on your land. What I do here and with whom, is no business of yours."

"You have made a grave mistake going against our understanding for the sake of this little *snake*," the Goddess sneered.

Medusa stood aghast. She had been raised praising the benevolent goddess. Now she stood scorned and defamed by her. She looked to the fountain in shame as tears streamed her cheeks.

"Athena, please." Poseidon's voice was calm. "You are overreacting. As the patroness of wisdom, you should see I have crossed no boundaries."

"Your mere presence on this plane is an infraction. I may be the goddess of wisdom, but I am also a proclaimer of warriors. This disrespect will not stand. She is mine! *I* took her in when your ilk rejected her." Athena glowered and then looked to Medusa who stood frozen in fear. The poor girl felt as though she might catch fire under the goddess's gaze. "You are a beauty—no mistake—but you dare to think yourself above my rules?" Athena's wrath was truly petrifying.

"No, my Goddess! I would never—" Medusa pleaded.

"You are but a toy to him!"

"Leave her out of this," Poseidon demanded.

"She *is* prettier than the last one you stole, I'll give you that." Medusa felt she might crumble to the ground. Could Poseidon have been using her to get to Athena?

"Leave us!" Poseidon roared, truly angered now.

Medusa stood shocked by the force in his voice. Even Athena seemed shaken, but she recovered quickly.

"You will be punished for this." Athena glared at Medusa.

"You would not dare," Poseidon warned.

"Wouldn't I?" The goddess's voice was ice.

"If you harm so much as a hair on her head—" The sky churned and grew dark, as if in response to his anger.

"You'll what?" she laughed. "She is mine and has been since she arrived here. You have no choice in her fate!" Athena took a short breath, calming herself. "However, I am not above mercy. I will not harm her as long as you agree to *never* interfere with her again." Athena's voice deepened. Her breathing slowed. "If you choose to betray our pact yet again—mark me—it will be she who pays the price. Now, son of Cronus, say your farewells to this slip of a girl. This is the only warning you will receive."

Medusa hardly glimpsed Athena's cold scowl before she disappeared.

Poseidon stood rigid a moment longer, only relaxing once he was sure Athena had truly left them.

"She is gone," Poseidon assured her, guiding Medusa into his arms. "She will not harm you."

Medusa felt naive suddenly. "So, you are Poseidon," was all she could think to say.

"I am sorry I did not tell you. I did not want to scare you," he told her softly.

"I think I already knew, or at least some part of me knew."

"I suppose you did," he replied with a slight smile.

"It doesn't matter to me who you are. If it turned out you were a great sea monster, I would still love you."

Poseidon stroked Medusa's pale cheek admiringly. "I am so sorry for this. I never dreamt she would follow me. Athena is jealous and vengeful, but if she says she will not harm you, she will not. Rest assured."

Medusa's smile faded as she recalled Athena's words. "She called me a 'toy.' What did she mean?"

Poseidon looked away then. "Medusa, I am older than this temple. I have had many lifetimes. This is one of the burdens of immortality. When one loves a mortal…they have a set amount of time."

"I see," she answered.

"Medusa, please believe me when I say I love you."

"I do," she replied sweetly. "But why did you come to me? I am nothing more than a lowly priestess. You, who has the very sea to command."

"Because you have enchanted me," he told her. "I have lied about nothing. Your song and your beauty are beyond that of any goddess."

"You must not say that."

"I will not lie."

Medusa's kiss was gentle. "Am I ever to see you again?"

Poseidon chose his words carefully. "If she catches me here again, she will make good her word. Though I am only partially here, and not on her land. Because of Morpheus's help, I have been able to appear to you in dreams."

"You mean, I am dreaming now?"

"Yes. I cannot reach you physically, not as long as you reside on Athena's island. However, there is one way."

"How?" Medusa asked, unable to mask the hope in her voice.

"My alliance with Selene. During the full moon she is at her most powerful. Unfortunately, with the preparations for the festival, Athena grew strong enough to sense me. If I could, I would take you away with me right now, but what she has said is true: being her priestess, I cannot just take you with me. That, Zeus would punish. It is complicated. However, if you were removed from this mortal coil, you would be beyond Athena's reach."

Medusa looked away sadly. "So, I would have to die."

"No, not at all dearest, you will be removed from this mortal land. With Selene's help, I can take you during the eclipse on the *Night of the Goddess*. It is a night unlike others. All gods are welcome to view and partake of the festival. Zeus decreed it so. That is why no one is to look into the eclipse. Any god who has a mind to can take a mortal and be within their right. This is what we will do. As soon as you are in my care, she cannot touch you."

Medusa sat considering his words, everything was happening so fast.

"It is also possible, because of your blood."

"I am not sure I understand."

"Have you not wondered how you arrived at this temple? About your origins? You are mortal, yes, but you are not human. Your beginnings lie in my domain—with the creatures of the sea. There are very few like yourself. You do not age as a typical mortal. You are truly a unique creature, my darling. Zeus cannot condemn you for returning to my province. It is Athena who will not allow you to go."

The truth played at the edges of Medusa's mind: the flowing forms she often glimpsed in the crashing waves, the absolute ease and comfort she felt while swimming along the island's shore. The mornings spent singing to the faces curling about her in the surf. She had been convinced these inviting sprites were simply figments of her imagination.

"That is why Athena said she took me in," Medusa reasoned. "My parents rejected me—my differences."

"Your form was more fitting in the human world. So they left you at the temple stair."

"Why did you never say?"

"Would it have made a difference to you if I had?"

Being raised under the tutelage of the Athenian priestesses, Medusa was taught to hold reason before feeling, but now she felt so flooded with emotion she did not know what to do or say.

"It is too much for you," Poseidon sighed, holding her tight.

"How will it be done?" There was newfound steel in Medusa's voice. "You would still be mine?"

"My love. I am yours already. The sorrow of never seeing you again far outweighs the sorrow of leaving this island forever."

Poseidon smiled down at her brightly, his eyes shimmering as though created from the sea itself. "It is agreed. Come the eclipse, I will take you away from here."

"We will be together."

"Yes. Forever. I will lay you on your own island where you may but flick your eyes to the sea and I will come to you. You shall be lavished with gifts, never want for anything. You will be mine and I will show you the mysterious depths of the sea itself. Places only I have seen."

"I require no gifts. Just you."

Poseidon smiled, but the curl of his lips faded quickly. "You are sure this is what you want, Medusa? My love. Once you go with me—"

"There is nothing for me here. I have never been more sure of anything."

"Then it will be done." In Poseidon's arms, all worry was washed from her. "On the *Night of the Goddess*, watch the eclipse and do not turn away. Selene will assist me in taking you."

They kissed and held one another until the sun rose, shattering their dream world. Poseidon bid her farewell, and though he was confident in their plan, Medusa could not shake the ominous feeling permeating the garden air.

Medusa was uneasy as she went about her chores. In past years, assisting the high priestess in readying for the *Goddess's Gala* was an all-consuming task, one which Medusa relished. This day, however, was blanketed in foreboding. At every turn, she felt daunted by the statues of Athena glaring down at her as she worked.

The night before, her dreams had been filled with terrible visions, visions of Athena's wrath should Medusa continue her meetings with Poseidon.

"What is the matter, child?" the high priestess called, startling Medusa. "You look terribly pale."

"I am sure it is nothing," Medusa replied, busying herself with arranging flowers in the vase before her.

"Perhaps you should lie down for a while. I will have one of the sisters finish your work."

"I am well, Priestess. Please do not concern yourself."

The high priestess nodded and turned to leave when Medusa heard her inhale sharply. Turning, she found the priestess staring up at the statue of Athena in horror.

"What is it, Priestess?" Medusa called, almost too nervous to ask.

"*Blood*," she replied in shock. "There is blood!"

Streams of red broke from the statue's eyes, trickling down the marble contours of its face.

"Athena weeps blood!" the high priestess wailed as she fell to the ground in supplication.

Medusa stood terrified—the weeping marble eyes bore into her own. Were Athena's tears of rage, or grief? Whichever they were, Medusa knew her transgression was the source—and she trembled in fear, there at the marble feet of the goddess of wisdom.

Soon all the priestesses in the temple gathered round, weeping and praying as they lay offerings at the foot of the statue.

The priestesses worked diligently to appease their angered goddess. They brought forth baskets of their choicest crops, anointed its pedestal with the finest perfumes, burned their most fragrant incense, and chanted their most revered songs and hymns. It was not until they drained the blood of their most virile ram that the statue finally ceased its weeping. No one in the temple knew the source of the goddess's anger. No one but Medusa.

After long preparation, the day of the *Gala* finally arrived. Medusa's heart fluttered and her fingers faltered as she readied herself for the ceremony.

In all the days before, her nightmares never truly left her—not even in her waking hours. They were a wretched plague causing her to wake screaming in the night, her mind wracked with visions of snakes, Thais in ruin, people slaughtered, and the expansive blue sky riddled with black clouds. She could not shake the horrible images, even now as she stared at the pristine and untarnished scenery outside her window.

Her hands grew clammy as she thought of all the night promised. Tonight she must decide to stay in the temple or leave with Poseidon forever. Unfortunately, Medusa knew she had little choice in the matter. Athena would never permit her to maintain her role as a temple priestess. Her only option was to leave. Though she truly loved Poseidon, the decision pained her: she could never return to the only home she'd ever known, never realize her dreams of becoming a high priestess. Medusa tried to be enthusiastic, but her nerves prevented her from truly reveling in this evening's many joys.

The door to her room flew open, startling Medusa from her somber thoughts. She was barely able to hide Poseidon's amulet beneath her robes before the high priestess flew in.

"Medusa, here you are! What is the matter with you, child? It is a most joyous day, come enjoy it with us!" Medusa had never heard the priestess so carefree—she all but sang as she spoke.

"I am sorry. I was just lost in thought," Medusa replied, her voice quavering.

"You are not feeling ill again, are you?"

"No, no, I'm fine," she replied uneasily. "Just relaxing before the ceremonies begin. You are in good spirits today." Finally looking up, Medusa was bowled over by the priestess's seemingly unshakable good mood.

"It is the night of the eclipse! How could I not be excited? The mighty goddess was merely testing our faith with her weeping statue. We are her favored once again!"

"Yes, it would seem so," Medusa replied half-heartedly.

"It is time we dance and sing! Time to rejoice!" The priestess grabbed Medusa's hand, pulled her to her feet, and twirled the girl in circles until she finally smiled. "That's it, Medusa, priestesses must inspire joy!"

Medusa spun out of their merry circle and dropped onto her bed. In doing so, Poseidon's amulet slipped from the neckline of her robe.

"What a lovely amulet." The priestess smiled, taking hold of it before Medusa could stop her. The high priestess froze as recognition flooded her face. "What is this?!"

"Nothing, Priestess."

"These are Poseidon's markings, Medusa! What have you done?" Medusa strained against the chain as the priestess tightened her grip on the amulet.

"I have done nothing. I swear it." Her voice was wracked with fear.

"I warned you against flirting with the gods! You have brought danger upon us all! Athena is not a forgiving goddess! You careless fool!"

The priestess ripped the amulet from Medusa's neck

and threw it to the ground. Medusa wailed as she lunged after it, but the high priestess stood firmly in her way.

"Please, he loves me!" Medusa sobbed at her feet.

"*Loves* you?!" the priestess scorned her. "Is that what you think?! Gods do not love! We are but pawns to them! Playthings!"

Tears flowed freely from Medusa's eyes. "He swore to me."

"Ignorance! Athena will raze our temple to the ground to get to you! I will not tolerate such defiance!" she screamed as she ripped at Medusa's ceremonial headdress.

Medusa shrieked as locks of golden hair were torn from her scalp.

"From this day forth, you are banished!" the priestess bellowed. Medusa clutched at her hair, whimpering as the high priestess loomed over her. "I will not have you upset the night's activities. You are not worthy of these ceremonies," she hissed. "You are to stay in your chambers. On the morrow, you will be sent from this island never to return. To think I once thought to call you daughter." The disgust in her voice bit into Medusa.

She sobbed desperately as the priestess left, slamming and locking the door behind her. Medusa ran to the window and looked out at her sisters preparing for the ceremony. The sun was setting and the eclipse, Medusa's only hope, would begin in a few short hours.

A sea of people gathered at the steps of the great

temple. The islanders held their breath in anticipation as the sun descended into the dull and lackluster sea. When the sun was finally extinguished, the dark sky hung clouded, as though readying for a storm.

The people waited for the warm winds to rise, the stars to shine, the light to skip across the sea. But the wind never stirred, the stars never gleamed, and the light never danced. The people of Thais were left alone in their uneasy silence. They could not ignore the sense of something ominous lurking on the horizon. "The goddess is displeased!" A voice rang out from amidst the crowd.

The panic spread until the crowd roared with fear.

Looking out from the towering steps of the temple, the high priestess knew exactly what caused her beloved goddess's displeasure.

"Calm, my people!" her voice rang out over the ensuing mob. "Someone has displeased our goddess. I know what must be done. The eclipse will take place and the festival will go on! Follow me and all will be well!"

The people cheered, rallied by the high priestess's confident words, and followed her into the temple.

Forlorn and bereft, Medusa stared out at the moon from her window, practically vibrating with anticipation. Eventually, the door to her chambers flew open and the priestesses she had once considered sisters—her friends—burst into the room, and dragged her roughly into the hall.

Medusa was pulled screaming down the ornate hallways of Athena's most majestic temple and tied between two pillars in the great room.

The priestesses and people of the island flowed into the hall in a tidal rush of anticipation, eager to catch a glimpse of the perpetrator. At first, the people of Thais could not comprehend what they saw. Before them hung their cherished Medusa—bound and trussed as if she were to be sacrificed. Murmurs of disbelief rippled through the hall.

"People of Thais! Here is the blight on our fair island!" the high priestess's voice carried, loud and clear, over the crowd. "Athena has punished us for this ignorant girl's lurid transgressions with her nemesis, Poseidon." Gasps of outrage circled through the crowd. "Tonight she will be punished. Athena will be appeased!"

The people roared their approval as one. Adored as Medusa may have once been, Thais would not risk the wrath of their terrible and beautiful goddess.

Medusa sobbed as she hung, painfully strung up by her arms. The eclipse was moments away but the people had blood on their minds. She had been so close to being with her love forever. Medusa prayed they would wait until the eclipse was full so Poseidon's power would be at its height and able to release her from this madness.

Time, however, was not on her side. The sky grew dark as the priestesses prepared a basin to catch Medusa's blood. However, none of the onlookers noticed the first dark sliver fall across the face of the moon. Had Selene somehow heard her plea?

Medusa watched as a young novice presented the

ceremonial dagger to the high priestess, who began the chanting required of a sacrifice. Her words echoed off the walls of the great room and the crowd chanted in unison. The anticipated bloodletting lifted their voices to a frenzied pitch. This would be the greatest *Goddess's Gala* ever witnessed.

Medusa's heart raced in terror as she glanced at the dagger approaching her chest. She began her own chanting: a beseeching prayer to Poseidon.

The shift in light was nearly imperceptible—yet it was enough to make the crowd turn from Medusa's sacrifice to the eclipsing moon. At that moment, the eclipse came to full cycle. Everyone, including the high priestess, bowed their heads away from the sight.

Except Medusa.

Eyes wide with relief, Medusa stared into the darkened face of the moon and felt herself lifted. Her heart leapt as the ropes unbound themselves and she floated, unhindered, away from the pillars. Her prayers had been answered.

Then, there was a jolting flash of light and Medusa fell roughly to the ground. She screeched in pain as her head and hands slammed into the cold marble floor. At her scream, every head in the hall jerked up from its reverent bowing. The high priestess glared and called for her priestesses to grab Medusa. Her yell was cut off by a hideous noise from the rear of the temple.

Turning, the islanders were appalled to see fissures crackling their way down the largest and most magnificent statue of their beloved Athena. The marble flaked and chipped, falling away to reveal a beautiful woman—fierce and more magnificent than anything the people of Thais had ever seen. Priestesses and villagers threw themselves to the ground in the presence of their mighty goddess.

Athena paid them no mind. "How dare you!" Her voice filled the hall and sank into the very hearts of the people, shaking the temple walls.

"Please! I meant no harm!" Medusa begged, terrified and pained as she looked up at the mighty Athena.

"You and Poseidon will pay for your insolence!"

Outside, the wind howled and the sea roared. Torrential rains soon drenched the smooth temple steps. A hurricane was brewing.

"I do not care how you roar, Poseidon! This is MY temple!" Athena's voice thundered strength and defiance. "Sink this island to the depths of the sea if you will, but this creature shall not be yours."

The high priestess threw herself at the goddess's feet, pleading for her to spare the temple. Athena only swatted her away, sending her flying into the temple wall. Athena's eyes never once left Medusa.

"I would kill you, but death is too good for such a treacherous snake!" The island itself trembled with the storm outside.

"No! Please!" Medusa begged—but there would be no mercy.

Athena thrust a hand forward, her eyes alight with power, and Medusa was pitched to the floor. There she screamed in agony as her flesh twisted upon her very bones.

People fleeing from the temple were immediately swept from the steps into the sea. Those who remained inside scrambled to the corners, praying to avoid the rampaging goddess's wrath.

Athena's laughs echoed and rumbled through the temple, causing the marble walls and statues to tumble upon the terrified worshipers.

On the temple floor Medusa continued to writhe. Her once alabaster skin grew patchy and rough as scales pushed to the surface. The flowing tendrils of her golden hair twitched and coiled, twining and untwining with a life of their own. Terrified, she now looked out through a tangle of long slim snakes. She felt her teeth elongate and curve into fangs. Her cries became even less decipherable as her tongue lengthened and forked. Panicked, she looked down to her legs upon the floor behind her. In their place lay a thick coil of green: scaly and sinuous in the torchlight. Medusa's screams were beyond sanity as she looked to her deformed figure in disbelief.

"You have all disgraced me by keeping this wretch!" Athena called, turning her wrath upon the women and girls of the temple. "You are no longer priestesses of mine!" With a twitch of her hand, the priestesses screeched in anguish and burst into flame. The people of Thais panicked anew as they beheld the ire of their goddess. They tried to run, but all were trapped between the clashing gods.

"A final touch for the fearsome gorgon." Athena's laughter was piercing as she turned her attention upon Medusa once more. Raising her hand to the wretched girl, Medusa's eyes were forced to look upon the enraged goddess. The second their gaze met, Athena disappeared.

Medusa's screams heightened as a searing pain exploded in her skull. She grasped and clawed at her eyes which felt afire, sure the goddess had stricken her blind. When the torture finally dissipated enough for her to open them again, she found her clawed hands drenched in blood. Medusa shrieked in panic as she searched the room for help, struggling to move her new horrifying body.

The same people who had once competed for a glimpse of Medusa now pushed and shoved one another to escape her presence. Medusa blindly lunged at a man, pleading for help, but when she looked at him, her terror turned to confusion: she was not holding a man, but a statue. There had never been a statue like this in the temple. Looking closer, she realized she recognized this man, she had seen him on many occasions in the village. Slowly, the truth took hold: the statue had once been a living, breathing man.

Throwing herself back in revulsion, Medusa stumbled to the floor, cracking her head on the unforgiving marble. The snakes crowning her brow nipped her face, hissing in anger. She slithered across the floor frantically, unable to control the direction. Everywhere she looked there were tumbled statues and fleeing people. Grabbing wildly for someone, anyone, she was consistently met with the unforgiving stone of statues. She screamed wildly as people ran from her, trampling one another and throwing themselves into the storm outside just to get away.

"Medusa! Where are you?" It was her Poseidon. "Come to me!"

Medusa sobbed and turned, in search of her love. But all that lay before her was a great puddle of water. "Poseidon?!" Medusa bellowed in her distress and clumsily slithered toward the water. Looking down, she was shocked to see Poseidon's likeness, blurry and undefined. "What has she done to me?!"

"Athena will pay for this!" His voice, watery and distant, was pure wrath. Medusa touched the water, but the vision only rippled away. "Where are you?"

Poseidon bowed his head in the settling reflection. "If I were to look at you in the flesh, I would be turned to stone, as all the others."

Medusa looked around at the terrifying statues surrounding her, all frozen in fear, all because of her. "How can that be?"

"The curse Athena has placed on you is forbidden by the gods. There is nothing I can do to remove it. She ensured we could never again be together."

"No!" Medusa had never experienced such agony. She buckled under the pain. With her body disfigured and her being shattered, Medusa's heart felt as though it would burst from the weight of such misery.

"Medusa, I must leave. I will see she is punished for this. Athena may be Zeus's favored daughter but this brazen misuse of our laws will not be ignored."

"Wait! Poseidon!" she cried, scratching frantically at the floor as the puddle dissolved. "Help me!"

"I am," he replied sadly and the waters dried up,

taking Poseidon with them.

"No!" she screamed, fumbling after the diminishing pool. He was gone. "Please! Don't leave me here! Don't leave me alone!"

The storm outside ceased and the sky cleared. Looking up to the moon, tears spilled from her horrible eyes.

Surely this was the end of her.

The next day Medusa awoke—bruised, battered, and beaten—on the steps of the temple. She tried to stand and quickly stumbled. Looking up from the horror of her body, she gave a cry at the sight of her surroundings.

"It can't be," she stammered.

The wreckage and devastation would haunt her nightmares forever. Above was a blanket of thick dark clouds, a pallid gruesome fog lingered in the air, bodies littered the shoreline, and the land was awash with broken flora. The dead strewn upon the temple steps were grey and bloated with sea water. In the night, most of the island had been consumed by the sea. Naught but a small patch of land surrounding the desolate temple remained.

Medusa wept as she pulled herself along the rubble-laden steps. There was not a soul left on the land.

Struggling to control her new serpentine tail, she used her arms to pull herself into the temple. She crawled over fallen statues, pillars, and the bodies of the dead to the center of the once great temple where she resigned to weep. All Medusa had wanted was to leave the island so she could live a life of love with

Poseidon. Now the island stood as an eternal testament to the death and destruction of all life on Thais.

All life but her own.

A year passed and Medusa saw nothing of Poseidon. She spent her days clearing the destruction of her temple and tending to what was left of the formerly magnificent gardens. Occasionally, as she worked she would discover an unbroken mirror and catch a glimpse of her horrible reflection. It was strange: though her skin had turned scaly and her golden hair transformed into a bouquet of ill-tempered serpents, her face had been left untouched. Despite the wretched changes wrought by Athena's wrath, she still had the same soft features, the same clear eyes and shapely cheeks—her face was still beautiful to behold. Medusa could not help but resent her unchanged features. No one could ever look upon her and live— her beauty was purely an added torment, a reminder of her former self.

In a fit of anger, Medusa smashed every mirror within the temple walls to obliterate every reminder of what had once been. However, when she came to the full-length mirror in her former chambers, she hesitated. The longing for her old life was too strong, too sharp. Medusa hung a long sheet over the thing and left it in peace.

She never entered that room again.

Over the days which stretched into months, the locked away mirror became a comfort to her; it was a symbol of her sanity. As long as she had the strength not to smash it, she knew there was something of her old self beneath her hideous serpentine shell.

Medusa often thought of the events leading up to her new life—if *life* was the name for this wretched existence. She had been such a fool. How could she believe Poseidon had really loved her? He told her he would take care of her and not once had she seen even the slightest sign of his return.

The only life remaining on Thais—aside from her self—was a small patch of garden. Though she grew bitter and depressed as the months stretched on, her small garden never failed to fill her with a sense of solace—to provide her a tiny moment of peace. The flowers did not turn to stone at her gaze. They had no eyes to see her.

Occasionally, adventurers from the mainland landed upon the shores of Thais. Medusa hid at first, fearful of the men looking to hunt her as game. As if she did not have enough heartache, now headhunters came in Athena's name, or simply for the prestige of killing a monster.

Medusa used her accursed stare to defend herself, but found as she tended her wounds that it could not be her sole means of survival. So, she harvested the weapons left by those she had killed: bows, swords, javelins, morning stars, anything intact. Deciding that close quarter combat was not for her, Medusa found archery the most appealing of her available defensive options. However, she worked to perfect her hand at each weapon all the same, readying for the next attack.

Thankfully, those who came for her head were ill-prepared to fight a beast such as she, and Medusa defeated them with little effort. Had they thought she would give up her head willingly? As disheartening and dismal as her days on the island proved, they continued to move forward; thus it came time again for the night of the lunar eclipse. It would be the first since the destruction. Medusa was not sure the eclipse would occur now that the gods had abandoned this place, but curiosity tempted her all the same.

She had slowly grown accustomed to her new body, and with relative ease, Medusa slithered through the halls of the temple, making her way across the cool marble floors to the garden. As she went, a glint caught Medusa's eye. She searched for its source and there, beneath a toppled pillar, lay the amulet Poseidon had given her. Medusa stared in disbelief. It was perfect, not a scratch on it, so unlike everything else in the temple. Including herself, she thought of her lost love, but did not weep. Medusa had shed all the tears she had for him, having wept a lifetime of tears in a single year. She considered tossing the beautiful thing away, but somehow could not bring herself to do so. Instead, she hung the gleaming charm around her neck and made her way to the garden.

Medusa coiled herself upon a low broken pillar in the midst of her flowers to gaze at the moon. She watched patiently, when to her surprise, a shadow crept across its silvery surface. Her heart fluttered slightly as she stared on, unblinking. She could not believe it had actually come. Some part of her—a not-so-small part—still hoped she might see Poseidon again. Despite her dismissed hopes, her heart raced as the moon grew dark and brilliant.

Medusa felt strange then as she stared into the moon, it was a pleasant and familiar sensation. Suddenly she heard a voice and her heart leapt anew. She looked to the garden wall; the voice came from behind the hedges. Medusa slithered quickly toward it, nearly stumbling with an excitement she couldn't control. She hurried through a maze of plants and flora which now extended far past the little acre of land she had been tending.

The hedges twisted and turned until she came to an ornate iron gate. Medusa had never seen such a gate before—it seemed wrought from moonbeams. She pushed it open and moved cautiously down a long aisle of tall shrubs, eventually spilling out into a fragrant and lush garden. There, in the center, was the fountain where she and Poseidon had met. Medusa spun in disbelief, her heart pounding. It was as beautiful as ever.

"Come to the fountain." The voice was muted and distant.

Medusa pulled herself onto the side of the fountain, unable to suppress the foolish hope she felt. "Poseidon?" she called, timid with sensations she thought lost.

Her voice sounded so foreign, having gone rusty and ragged with lack of use. She heard the waters ripple from the fountain, and hoping he was there, hoping to embrace him, she turned to it.

In the fountain's water alone was her love's perfectly reflected face.

"My darling Medusa," Poseidon's voice rang through the waters.

"Where have you been? Why did you leave?" She was unable to keep the wrath from her voice.

"I could not come back to you until now," he replied sadly. "It was difficult to find a way to see you. I can only look upon you with Selene's help and the protection of these waters," he told her. "No one can survive your sight: mortal or immortal. The gods have determined you too great a danger to be freed. I prevented them from sinking the island entirely."

"What do I do?" Her plea was nearly a wail.

"You must stay here, for eternity," he replied shamefully. His helplessness and anger caused the waters of the fountain to froth.

"Here?!" Her heart sank in despair.

"Athena has been punished many times over. For her insubordination, Zeus has even taken away her ability to bear children," he replied, but this was no comfort to Medusa.

"What will happen to me?"

"I wish I knew, my sweet."

"Is there nothing you can do? Are you not a god?!" she cried desperately.

"Once a curse is placed, it cannot be reversed."

"But you must take me away from here! I cannot stand it!"

"I am sorry, my love. Zeus demands you stay here. As lord of the gods, his word is law. You will live here, like this. Until the end of time."

Medusa choked on her ire. To spend eternity on this

desolate, lifeless island. "How can this be?!" Her reptilian eyes watered for the first time in months and she found she had not shed *all* her tears, as she had thought.

"I will find a way for us to be together," Poseidon soothed her.

Medusa laughed bitterly. "How could you want me anymore? I am hideous!"

"Though I cannot look upon you in person, I can see you," he replied softly. "Your golden locks and porcelain skin are gone, but your face, Medusa, is beautiful as ever. Your soul will never be tarnished in my eyes."

Medusa wanted to scream, wanted to cry, wanted to tell him he was foolish for seeing her as anything but a monster.

"Will you sing for me?" His voice was full of the same fervent adoration as the first time he had made the request.

Medusa stared to the broken stone flooring of the garden. "I cannot."

"Please, Medusa. Sing for me." The tenderness in his voice cut through her like a knife.

She could hardly speak anymore, let alone sing. But she could not bear to deny Poseidon. Reluctantly, she attempted to sing. It took time to figure how to form the melody with her forked tongue. She began with a series of hisses which slowly turned to words. After a few frustrated moments, her voice flew out over the gardens—as full and rich as ever.

"You are still enchanting." Poseidon's smile was

heavy with admiration. Medusa sang for him until the dark sky grew light.

"I am afraid I must go now," he told her.

"Will I ever see you again?" Medusa asked, terrified of the answer.

"On the nights of the full moon, my love. I will come to hear you sing," he replied.

"But once a month?" she sighed in disappointment.

"It is the night the moon shines brightest and the waters are at their clearest."

Medusa stared at the waters of the ornate fountain, attempting to memorize every beloved detail of his face. "Until then," she replied sadly.

"A parting gift, my sweet," Poseidon added to her surprise, and disappeared from the waters.

Looking up, she found herself surrounded by lush greenery, the small patch of growth around her having expanded and tripled. Her sad little plot had turned into a beautiful and exotic garden bursting with flowers of every kind and color.

"Until the next moon," Poseidon's soothing voice called once more and was gone.

Poseidon, as promised, appeared every night of the full moon, looking up from the fountain as Medusa sang. It was the only bright moment in her dark world.

Medusa continually marveled at how much she missed the contact of others—the touch of a hand, casual conversations with patrons, the camaraderie she had shared with the other priestesses. This dreary life continued month after month, year after year. Her only joy was in sitting beside the fountain to gaze upon a love she would never again hold. She grew strong, ruthless, resilient, and stayed as such. Except in those few hours when she closed her eyes and was allowed to live as she had once, dancing next to the sparkling light of the silvery fountain with her love.

And so, there was no one left to remember the beautiful young girl who had once been so adored and cherished by her people; so lovely the gods themselves envied her. All that remained was a story which took shape on the mainland. Mothers told their children, generation after generation, of Medusa, the fearsome snake-haired gorgon, who—peeking from beneath her hair of hissing, writhing asps—would turn a man to stone with one thoughtless bat of her terrible eye.

~~~~

Killian raised his eyes, but the mist did not dissipate as expected. Again the brothers' eyes turned black, their gazes suddenly pulled to the heart of the tree.

Phantom images appeared: a woman residing upon a throne of bones beside a man in black. Their eyes a deep, depthless black. Black as the inky darkness that enveloped them.

The image swiftly shifted to the dark-eyed woman standing before a great black pit in the middle of a desert, the sun beating down upon her reflected back in waves of heat and smoke. From within the darkness before her, a voice cried out in warning—a warning unheard by the watchers, but felt all the same.

The brothers' heads snapped back. The orb grew opaque and the darkness cleared from their eyes.

"Another warning?" Patrick could not keep the worry from his voice.

"I know that girl," Angus muttered in surprise. "She belongs to Romulus."

"And I recognize the man looming behind her," Banon added. "He is the benefactor to our ship."

"What does this mean?" Killian asked.

"Better to ask those in the vision, I imagine," Patrick replied.

"This eye tells the future, sometimes the present, and only rarely the past," Angus told them. "What we saw hasn't happened. Asking the people within the image will only confuse them. This girl's been shown before. The Fates seem to watch her every move."

"She looked common enough. Then again, appearances are often deceiving," Killian contemplated.

"The girl played a vital role in our recent war," Angus told them. "Not much time has passed and already she appears to me again. It's time to act."

"Careful, Brother," Killian warned. "You'll play right into the Fates' hands."

"Nothing we can do will ever truly affect their decision," Angus replied. "Going against my instincts to act would only make matters worse."

The brothers looked to one another uneasily.

"Let's get on with it, then." Angus said tensely. "Banon? Do you have another tale?"

"I do," he replied, digging in his pockets. After a moment he pulled out a shimmering claw—long, thin, and deathly sharp. "I offer another tale of a man newly introduced to the world of the supernatural. I sacrifice the talon of a sea creature who nearly had the opportunity to bury this very claw deep into the throat of this story's hero."

Banon placed the talon upon the great oak table. There, it grew translucent as it began to liquefy.

THE DEATH CALL

It was a particularly dull stint of the voyage. With the calm weather and smooth seas, very little effort was needed to keep their course. They were headed northeast, and had been for nearly two days now. The winds were calm and amiable, the sea had but the slightest ripples, and the sun hung high. It was perfect napping weather for the crew and everyone took full advantage. He couldn't understand what could possibly have McBain up in arms.

"Captain says we're in for some troublesome..." Jonathan called as he reached Knox at the wheel.

"You don't know the half of it," Knox growled, keeping a wary eye on the horizon.

"May I ask what it is? The trouble, I mean."

"You'll see soon enough. Just do as you're told and you should come out fine."

"Yes, Sir," Jonathan had grown accustomed to these vague responses. Though whether they were intended for keeping the crew from panicking or the sick joy of watching them squirm with curiosity, he could never be sure.

The captain had warned them of difficulties on their horizon but no one aside from Knox seemed anxious. Other than showing her face for morning announcements and holding a brief meeting or two, McBane had stayed in her quarters. Jonathan thought it a shame she refused to join them on deck for some sun. It wasn't in her nature, though, to loll about with the crew. He desperately longed to speak with her about things past—but in these long months, there never seemed to be a moment alone with her, and he dared not speak of such things in front of the crew.

Once Jonathan had his fill of sun, he decided to join Knox at the helm. Since their encounter with Lido, Knox had been sure to keep Jonathan included in the plotting and navigation of their trip. Though neither he nor the captain gave Jonathan much clue as to *why* they were traveling to any specific destination—just the tide tables, maps, and a general heading.

Jonathan headed to the aft cabin to double check their route when something in the distance caught his eye. It wasn't anything spectacular; it might have gone unnoticed if not for the fact that there had been *nothing* for days. A thin, dark ribbon sat on the horizon and stretched as far as the eye could see in either direction. Jonathan consulted his maps: they were quite some distance from the rocky barrier ahead, but the fact that it was already visible astounded him. How large could the barrier possibly be?

As they sailed closer, Jonathan refused to believe what he saw: the rocks ahead weren't just rocks, they were veritable mountains, standing in a long line, impenetrable and impervious to the crashing of the sea. In either direction the mountains spanned, seeming to go on forever. It was an impossible notion, but Jonathan had never seen anything like it. The entire crew had gathered near the bow to stare at the wonder.

Squinting, he could just make out the lethally sharp points and ridges of the jagged mountains when the captain appeared on deck. The crew snapped to attention, but she only nodded at Knox to follow her below deck.

The crew stood in confusion as the ship neared a great break in the rocky face; it was time to man their stations, but no orders were given. The men just swayed with the rolling of the ship and waited. A few moments later, their confusion deepened as Knox and the captain emerged with armfuls of bandages.

"Take one of these cloths and bind your ears," McBane commanded, much to the bewilderment of the crew. "After, tie your lifelines and report to your stations." The captain's voice dropped an octave as she looked hard at the men before her. "You are ordered to keep your bandages in place. No matter what you see, or think you hear. This order stands until you're personally instructed by either me or Mr. Knox to remove the wrappings. Is that clear?"

Bewildered, the crew's "Aye, Captain!" was brisk and immediate.

"Keep your heads up, stay steady, and watch for my signals," she continued. "We *will* make it through this unscathed."

Knox and McBane ensured that every man had tied his bindings firmly. Jonathan tried to ask what was happening, but Knox's lips were set in an uncharacteristic grim line. Curious, Jonathan watched as Knox secured his own bindings and the captain checked them.

All was eerily still as they continued toward the cliffs, trussed up in their peculiar restraints. He didn't see why the lifelines were necessary. While the sky above was certainly grey, the weather was perfectly calm and still with just enough of a breeze to billow their sails, bringing them closer to the rocky cliffs.

Now that the *Persephone* was close enough, Jonathan could see they would have little trouble navigating this pass: they could sail between the soaring cliffs with ample room on either side of the hull.

The crew held their puzzled silence as they drew closer to the cliffs—cliffs which grew more looming and menacing with each passing moment. The reason for the lines soon became clear, but not the bandages. Why wouldn't she just tell them what was happening? The sea bashed against the rocks with such ferocity it was a wonder they did not shatter. In some places along the land, the water pooled into dangerous sinkholes. Should they hit even one, they would be hard-pressed to get out again without crashing into the jagged rocks. It wasn't an ideal path, but they had sailed through far worse.

The sea air hung heavy around them, still and stagnant. Luckily, it was just enough to keep them headed through the treacherous divide.

Time slowed as they sailed at little more than a drift—their surroundings only growing bleaker as they continued on. Soon, a faint fog rolled across the water, making it difficult to see the rocks which jutted up from the water like claws. Knox's knuckles were white on the helm as he squinted into the fog.

It was a tedious trek but there was an end in sight.

Jonathan looked down at the sharp bits of stone protruding from the sea to discover they weren't all stone. Some were wood with tays and ropes around their base. These weren't rocks, but wrecks. Like icebergs, the greater parts of their broken hulls and masts lay beneath the fog and water.

Looking ahead, more ships hulls could be seen. A chill ran down Jonathan's spine. Strange trees grew all around, springing up from the water like thin white arms. These stark formations in actuality were *bones*, piled high and held together with bleached sinew. The crew stared on in horror. However, the captain only looked ahead, signaling every now and then on which direction the sails should turn.

Reluctantly turning his attention back to the *Persephone*'s bow, Jonathan struggled to decipher what he was seeing: halfway up the rocks ahead he noticed three thin white lines upon the cliff face. Atop each line was a smudged blot: one red, one black, one gold. He could not turn away as the ship grew level with this newest oddity. Then he realized each smudged blot was actually a head attached to the body of a woman *floating* against the sinister cliff face.

McBane stood unfazed by these creatures and continued calmly signaling the crew.

Though startling and unnatural, the beauty of these three women was undeniable. They looked down on the crew with their arms open in welcome. Were they angels of the sea guiding sailors through this rocky channel? Jonathan saw their lips mouthing words down at the crew. For a moment, he forgot the bindings around his ears.

Glancing back, yet again, he saw the stern set of the captain's jaw as she glared up at the shimmering women. It then dawned on him that *they* might be the danger McBane guarded against.

McBane turned suddenly, concern etched upon her face. Jonathan followed her gaze to one of the men below who had wandered to the edge of the ship, his ear bindings half off, stretching his lifeline as far as it would reach.

Knox was busy at the wheel and the captain had to direct the crew. Jonathan knew he had to help.

With a nod to the captain, he untied his own lifeline from the railing and headed down the quarterdeck stair to the man straining desperately toward the three mesmerizing forms. The man's bindings now hung loosely around his neck as he pawed mindlessly at the knot of his lifeline. Jonathan quickly refastened his own lifeline to the lower railing and turned, trying to get the man's attention. No matter what he did, the crewman paid him no mind.

Jonathan looked back to the captain who motioned for him to cover the man's ears. Catching on, Jonathan rewrapped the man's head. But the sailor suddenly flailed in protest, knocking him back. Annoyed, Jonathan continued his struggle only to receive a nasty blow to the side of his head. Jonathan's world tilted and his ears rang as he grasped at the man.

Then, he heard it.

Singing.

Dumbstruck, he locked eyes on the women above. Their song pulled at him like nothing he'd ever known. They sang such sweet notes: songs of far off seas he'd never before heard; songs of longing and desire; songs of promise and songs of triumph.

Their beauty filled his vision: he saw distant unexplored lands with great vast oceans leading to the heavens. Stars hung so tightly packed, he could not hope to ever count them. He walked across glassy pools of gently churning water. Jonathan needed no boat to explore; he was free, free to roam wherever he wished. The seas were his to command. The stars begged to tell him the very secrets of existence.

Suddenly and painfully, these infinite lands of euphoria were wrenched from his grasp. Agony wracked his mid-section as he looked down upon jagged rocks and crashing waves.

Jerkily, he was pulled back. McBane stood above

him, checking his bindings and retying his life line. When had it come undone?

Jonathan blinked at his surroundings. He stood at the railing, drenched with seawater, and aching all over. The ship's port side hugged the jagged space between the cliffs, rocking back and forth, nearly hitting sinkhole after sinkhole. An ill-tempered gust of wind now blew. All around, the crew fought to keep the sails taught and the ship on course.

Wincing, Jonathan got to his feet and sprinted to the helm to assist Knox, who struggled with the wheel.

Working tirelessly, they sailed straight through the center of the great cliffs—all eyes were downcast, all bindings firmly wrapped. Finally, the cliff walls broke and the *Persephone* was in open waters yet again. They had escaped their would-be grave.

Thankful to be alive, but desperately restless, Jonathan wanted to turn back. He needed to return to the stunning land he'd only briefly glimpsed, needed to skim the starry waters of those distant lands. It took him some time to realize he was pulling at the helm, struggling against Knox's steering. Shaking uncontrollably, he released the wheel and dug his fingers into his hair as he tried to push the visions away.

"Take a break, Maritime," Knox quietly commanded, his eyes full of pity.

Jonathan only nodded and went to the deck to assist in belaying ropes.

Slowly, the crew shrugged out of their lifelines and ear wrappings, like snakes sloughing off old skins.

They blinked and shook their heads as though waking from a dream.

Once they were on a steady course, Jonathan approached the captain. "What happened back there?"

"*Sirens*. I've dealt with them before," she replied as she nodded to Knox and headed past him down the stair to her quarters.

Jonathan pursued. "Is that why you didn't need the ear bindings? I saw things back there. What happened, what did I see?"

"I wouldn't know, but Knox has been through it. It is said their songs reveal your deepest heart's desire. Perhaps you can ask him sometime."

"When did you encounter these creatures?" Jonathan asked and couldn't help what he would say next. It had been bottled up far too long and he was too weak to keep it at bay. "Was it before or after you rescued me from servitude?"

Moira froze just before reaching her door and turned back to Jonathan. Moving close to him, she looked him straight in the eye. "We rescued each other, and I thank you not to speak of such times again."

"Why?" Jonathan asked, despite his better judgment.

"The woman you knew no longer exists," she replied in a fierce whisper. "Be aware, it is no longer the same person you address."

Jonathan stared back, surprised by her coldly rigid countenance. "I think you're right," he replied. "That Moira would have warned me of danger, would have warned her crew."

"You had what you needed to know. Would you, or any of the crew, have believed we were to encounter Sirens?" Jonathan could only shake his head. "Is that all, crewman?"

"Yes, Ma'am," he replied through tight lips.

She turned quickly, disappearing into her chambers. For the first time, Jonathan wondered just what he had gotten himself into by boarding the *Persephone*.

~~~~

Banon closed his misty eyes. When he reopened them, they had returned to their blond-brown shade. The small liquid pool left by the siren's claw quickly evaporated into the great stump.

"Is there a place your ship has *not* sailed?" Killian asked his brother.

"We've been everywhere from here to the depths of Tartarus itself."

"Another good tale," Angus commented distractedly, gazing at the door of the great room.

"What is wrong, Brother?" Killian asked.

"I'm beginning to doubt Conner will show."

"He may have an easily distractible eye but he would never miss a Social Ball."

"I hope you're right. If he doesn't show we'll be a story short and I have no other tales for the offering."

"I have another story in the meantime. A lighthearted piece," Patrick offered.

"Go ahead, Brother. Let us just hope Conner shows before the sun rises."

The brothers nodded to Patrick who then pulled a small wooden box from his pocket and slid the top open. "I offer this tale of a young man in the grips of changing youth who attempts to exact revenge upon his peer. I bring the tools of his revenge."

Patrick turned the box over and several very small, very white, very dead bugs fell onto the table, where their husks instantly began to brown.

THE OTHER CHARMING BOY

Ash ran through the halls of Legends Primary as though his life depended on it, which was very possible. If his plans headed south, Domino Charming was sure to have him strung up by his shoelaces. However, Ash would *not* entertain thoughts of failure.

He fingered the secret weapon in his jacket as he smuggled it into the cafeteria and through the sterile dining hall, avoiding eye contact with the other students. This was the gauntlet. If he could make it to his table at the back of the hall without attracting attention from the Odd Kids, the Valiants, or the Charmings, he would be home free.

Ash kept his eyes to the floor as he passed the

Weird table, a motley crew of frightening students who kept to themselves. If you were unlucky enough to anger them, their ringleader, Brody Wicked, would stick you in a trashcan and be done with you. Ash breathed easier once he passed them, though they were the least of Ash's worries. Bruises were easily suffered—it was the public ridicule the Charmings loved to dole out that he couldn't handle.

Out of the corner of his eye, Ash spotted the Valiants' table. They were the children of the Valiant brothers, a soldiering family whose great deeds had earned them lands, titles, and fair maidens. They were stuck-up and stern, but kept to themselves when not in competition with the Charmings. He stifled a gasp as he caught a glimpse of Samba Valiant, his long-time crush. He had never actually spoken to the girl, but would someday have the courage to ask her out.

Someday.

Ash passed the table, ignoring the snickering comments the children of the Valiant brothers made under their breath. Now, he began to sweat. If he got past his abusive cousins, the Charmings, all would be well. The Charmings were the children of those princes who won fair damsels and defeated magnificent monsters. Their renown and desirability was of mythical proportions.

The only benefits Ash had gained from being a Charming were a square jaw and a head of thick hair. No premature balding for him. It was his mother's side of the family that had provided the bad skin and gangly structure. Puberty was *not* being kind. "Ugly

Duckling Syndrome," his mother had called it. Privately, he called it the "Only-Half-Charming Syndrome."

He was bitter toward his cousins. They were rich—filthy rich—members of the richest family in the Kingdom. Ash's parents on the other hand, though holding the title, had no fortune to speak of. His father, Sue Charming, had rebelled from the Charming family, refusing to take part in their deeds, lands, and sizable fortune. He married Ash's mother, Cindy Rella, and though Cindy was a beauty, she had no dowry to speak of.

Ash continued past his horrible relatives to sanctuary, the table at the back of the hall where his childhood friend, Harper Beanington, and their sometimes lunch buddies, Hattie and Horatio Hatter, were already halfway through their meals. Ash slid into the seat across from Harper and looked over his shoulder to make sure he hadn't awoken any suspicions.

"Where have you been? Lunch is nearly half over," Harper asked, genuinely concerned. Being Ash's best friend, she knew the abuses he faced at the hands of his cousins.

Ash changed the subject. "Where's Rayne?"

"She's with her dad, you know that. Now why are you looking so guilty?" Harper asked.

"Yeah, Ashley, why are you hunched over the table and what are you hiding in your jacket?" Hattie asked, her inquiries born more from curiosity than concern.

"It's a secret, and I told you before, don't call me

Ashley."

"You're keeping a secret?" Harper asked doubtfully as she swept her thick golden hair out of her bronze face.

"Not from you, from *them*," Ash replied, nodding back at the Charming table. "Today, my friends, is the day I exact revenge on Domino for all the pranks he's played on me."

"What, like the time in the locker room when he replaced your shampoo with a coloring spell?" Horatio offered.

Harper sighed. "It was such a lovely shade of violet."

"Or the time Domino wedgied you in front of Samba." Hattie laughed.

"Or when he knocked you in the fountain."

"Or—"

"Yes." Ash cut them off. "All that. Thanks for the reminders."

"Okay then, what's the plan this time?" Horatio asked. "Exploding potatoes like last week? Or attack pixies like the week before?"

"The pixies were adorable." Harper smiled reminiscently.

"Yes, but they just danced around, stealing everyone's breadcrumbs. Not much of an attack." Hattie giggled.

Ash smiled as he set a small box wrapped in polka-dot paper on the table before them.

"You're going to give him a present?" Harper asked confused.

"It's not *really* a present. It's a trick," he whispered. "Soon as Domino opens this, it's going to release pigment bugs."

"Pigment bugs? Where did you get those?"

"You know how Mom is. She keeps all sorts of creatures around the house. Found them when we were cleaning out the shed. Anyway, it'll be amazing. Domino will open the box, the bugs will get all over him, and they'll eat away that tan he works so hard on. He'll be white as a ghost for weeks!"

"That's it?" Harper asked. "You're going to ruin his tan?"

"It's perfect," Ash insisted. "Diamond and Domino have skin white as snow like their mom. He has to tan every other day to keep his color. He complained about it every time our parents made us play together. It's the perfect revenge for the purple hair."

"Violet," Harper corrected.

"Yeah that's great, Ash. Just one problem," Horatio replied. "How are you going to get him to open it?"

This stopped Ash short. "I was going to hand it to him."

"Don't you think that's a bit suspicious?" Harper asked.

"Well, how else do I get it to him?"

"I don't know." Horatio chuckled. "It's *your* master plan."

Ash sat stumped. Domino not opening the box had never factored in. "Well," Ash told them, "If he doesn't want to open it, I could put it in his locker."

"The anonymous package thing is probably a better

route," Hattie replied.

"Plan B if he doesn't open it," Ash affirmed.

Harper shook her head. "But then he'll know it's from you and the second plan won't work either."

"I'll rewrap it!"

"Domino is pretty dumb, but even he's not going to fall for that," Horatio scoffed doubtfully.

"Ash isn't going to listen." Harper chuckled. "He's got it in his head. Go exact your revenge. We're watching."

Ash looked like he would explode with excitement at any moment. Quickly he took his dastardly present and headed toward the Charmings' table. Every step felt like an eternity as he advanced on his nemesis.

After about a year, he found himself at the edge of his cousins' table.

"Can I help you?" Diamond asked coldly.

Ash had planned something witty to say upon handing over the box, but his mind was a blank as he held the box toward Domino.

Domino looked up at it, a disbelieving sneer on his face. "Is that supposed to be for me?"

Ash nodded, praying he would take the package and let him go back to his table to watch the mayhem from a safe distance. Domino continued to sneer, but reluctantly took the package.

Ash quickly turned to leave.

"Aren't you going to at least watch him open it?" Diamond asked suspiciously.

"I can see fine from my table."

"I insist you stay," Domino replied. In an instant,

his larger cousins, Zed and Ted, towered on either side of Ash.

Ash could only stand stunned. He was going to be beaten to a pulp in front of the entire school, but it would be worth it to get back at Domino. He had nearly opened one side of the package, when his sister stopped him.

Ash's heart sank.

"I would hate to think that our dear cousin Ashley might give you something harmful, but we should take a precaution," she smiled cunningly.

"Precaution?" Ash choked.

"Just a simple spell," Diamond replied and placed her hand on the package where she mumbled a few words. "There." she smiled.

"Thanks, Sis," Domino replied and continued opening the package.

As soon as he opened it, tiny white bugs streamed toward Domino's hands. Ash watched excitedly. But something was wrong. The bugs suddenly changed direction and headed back to Ash.

"I love the 'Return to Sender' spell." Diamond laughed as the bugs crawled up Ash's leg. "It repels malicious deeds, sending them back on whoever dispatched them."

Ash tried to back away, but Ted and Zed held him in place as the bugs burrowed into his pores.

"Pssst," Ash called to the chipmunks on the branch next to him. "Come chew these laces will you?"

The chipmunks just laughed and ran deeper into the tree. He hung from his shoelaces dismally. He could talk to animals, sure, but getting them to do what he wanted was another thing altogether.

"*There* you are," Harper called. Ash looked down at her from the tree in the center of the courtyard. "Next time, just put the box in his locker," she told him, scaling the tree.

"Duly noted," he groaned.

"So how long is your skin going to stay white?" she asked as she unknotted his laces.

"About a week."

"That's not so bad." Harper's voice was cheerful. "They tied these things pretty good though. I'm going to have to cut them." She sighed as she rifled through the art supplies in her bag.

"Alright," Ash groaned. "Just let me know when you're about to—" Before he could finish, his laces snapped and he plummeted to the courtyard.

"So, have you learned your lesson?" Harper asked as she came down the tree and helped him to his feet.

"Yes," Ash replied. "Next time I'll use a long-range surprise attack. Up close and personal clearly doesn't work."

Harper shook her head as she escorted her albino friend to their next class. "Well, Rayne and her dad had to cut their trip short, so at least we'll have a good story for her when we get to Round Table Café."

"Yea, I'm sure she'll love it," he replied distractedly as he began spinning new schemes to get back at Domino.

~~~~

The mist cleared from Patrick's eyes as the husks dissolved into dust.

"Such strange people reside in your land," Angus observed.

"They are called pubescent males and I believe they exist everywhere. You are more removed from the world than I thought." Patrick could not help but chuckle.

"Yes, yes. I understand I need to leave my home now and again. Banon," he called turning the conversation away from himself. "Do we have another from your navigator?"

"I certainly do, but I am running out of my prepared offerings. Let us hope Conner shows soon." With that, Banon removed a thin piece of wood from his coat pocket, the kind used for constructing cargo crates, and held it before the dark eye. "I offer this old tale of a young man who can find his way on a starless night, yet finds himself hopelessly lost to a world of dark creatures."

Banon placed the wood upon the old oak where it began to warp and puff.

AT MIDNIGHT

Jonathan had a strange feeling about the large box the ship picked up that night. They had brought unmarked cargo aboard many times but never quite such a large container, and never so late.

Finishing up his work on the next day's charts, Jonathan found himself overly distracted by the crew as they carefully loaded the crate below decks. Once it was stowed out of his sight, he felt more at ease. However, a lingering curiosity burned in his mind.

The *Persephone*'s scheduled course was relatively simple but every month or so she'd take a detour. Whenever they picked up one of these strange parcels, their next destination would always be somewhere–

exotic. Jonathan had grown accustomed to this unspoken ritual, but the delivery of the previous package had led the *Persephone* and her crew to the base of a volcano inhabited by pygmies. The parcel before that had taken them to a glacier the size of a small island run by strange ice creatures. He had thought the ice creatures merely small humans in strange garb, but upon seeing their eyes, he knew they were something—else.

These stops never failed to send a strange thrill of excitement up Jonathan's spine. He even found himself looking forward to the next adventure the detours were sure to bring.

Unlike the other packages, however, this one exuded an energy all its own, causing Jonathan to worry about their next destination.

"Mr. Maritime," Captain McBane called from the door to the navigation room. "We have our heading. I trust you will be able to decipher this map?"

The captain handed him a dark cloth slashed with deep red markings. The legend of this oddly embroidered map was written in a language he did not understand; yet there were many similarities between those markings and a standard navigational chart. The first word that sprang to his mind was *demonic*. The compass rose even bore a strong resemblance to a pentagram. Though it still depicted north-south directional markings. "I'll get it drawn up as soon as I can, Moira," he replied, continuing to study the strange map.

Instead of leaving, the captain stood silent. Jonathan

immediately realized he had accidentally used her first name. Moira sighed, closed the door to the cabin, and leaned against Jonathan's desk.

"I'm sorry," Jonathan apologized. "I should not have used your first name."

"No, I am sorry," she replied to his surprise. "When I brought you aboard this ship all those months ago, I thought twice about it." Jonathan's heart sank. Did she regret hiring him? "It's not because of you," she assured him. "It is our mutual past. I hoped I could ignore it, that in time it would be forgotten, but I see now that this is an impossibility. It frustrates us, and in our line of work we need to have clear heads. I still have no desire to discuss the past with you, nor will I elaborate on my journey between then and now. It is my business and my business alone."

"I apologize again, Captain," Jonathan replied sadly.

"However, when not in front of the other crewmen, you may refer to me as you like, as long as it is respectful. In memory of your sacrifice in that time. I have not forgotten my debt to you."

"You owe me nothing."

"I may have died in that forest if not for your help and direction. That is not a debt I take lightly. This ship is your home as long as you wish it. And though I know this is not the sort of heart-to-heart you were looking for, it is the only one I am able to offer you. Do you understand?"

"Yes, ma'am," Jonathan replied. It was the most she had opened up to him. Unfortunately, he had the feeling it would be the last time in a long while.

"It is just the two of us. Call me Moira," the captain corrected.

"Thank you, Moira."

With that she stood and headed to the door. "I await your coordinates," she called over her shoulder and was gone.

With a somewhat lighter heart, Jonathan set to work on a basic heading before retiring for the night.

The oddities of the strange cloth map haunted Jonathan's dreams, along with the crooning of an alluring voice.

It was still dark when he awoke to the sound of his name.

He sat up in his bed. "Who's there?"

No one answered.

Sure it must have been a dream, he laid back down, only to be awoken again. Reluctantly Jonathan pulled on his breaches and made his way to the door of the cabin. He peeked out to the deck. Only the lookout high up in the crow's nest was about. He turned to the navigation room to discover a faint glowing upon his desk. In the dim moonlight, the scarlet markings of the dark map glimmered with an eerie light.

"Jonathan," the voice called to him again, louder now.

It was definitely coming from outside the room.

Jonathan pulled on his overcoat and followed the voice onto the deck and to the stairs of the hold. The calling led him down into the hull. Once there, he wondered if he should wake Knox, or perhaps even Moira. But Jonathan walked on as though in a dream. He meandered down into the galley, not really knowing where he was going until he stood in the cargo hold, staring at the cargo they had brought aboard that evening.

Suddenly, the atmosphere around him tightened. His breath hitched in his chest as the air around him grew dense. He flinched as this denseness was suddenly torn with a shrill squeal, followed by a bang and a resonating crack. He wanted to run, more than anything, but he was rooted to the dank planks beneath his feet.

With a shudder, the lid to the crate lifted then gently slid to the side and onto the floor where it landed with a thud. He gaped at the gently swirling fog which lingered within the box. However, the next thing he saw astonished him more than anything he'd ever seen: more than the pygmies of the volcano or the creatures of the iceberg.

A lady's hand, ghostly pale with long curling fingernails, emerged from the fog to grip the side of the wooden crate. Slowly, the figure of a dark-haired woman rose. Another excited thrill ran down Jonathan's spine as the specter, shrouded in a cryptic loveliness, slowly turned toward him. Her face was porcelain white and impossibly smooth, her neck long and delicate. Her shoulders were nearly bare, covered only by the shreds of a musty linen undergarment. The woman's eyes were a deep amber. Try as he might,

Jonathan could not turn away.

"Who are you?" he managed.

"A friend," she replied, her husky voice dark yet sweet. "I wish to know you. Come closer, Jonathan." She raised one perfectly formed leg and placed her foot upon the crate's edge.

He felt himself compelled forward. "How do you know me?"

"I hear you above, I feel your presence, sense your essence. You were close to a piece of my home land. I miss it."

"The map, you mean?"

Suddenly he found himself next to the crate, leaning toward the woman who lightly dragged her fingers across his cheek, around his jawline, and back into his hair, gently pulling him into her embrace. Jonathan's heart pounded with excitement. He was blind to all but the simmering of her gilded amber eyes.

He dared not even breathe as he stared on, enchanted by the perfect lips poised inches from his. Mesmerized, he did not notice the long piece of sharp steel until it was over his shoulder.

"Your fangs break skin and I will personally throw you off this vessel. Consequences be damned," Captain McBane warned the woman in Jonathan's arms.

The creature loosened its grip just enough for Jonathan to pull back and see the viciously sharp fangs protruding from the woman's lips.

"But I'm so hungry." Her mouth was still just inches from the blood—now pounding fiercely—in Jonathan's jugular.

"You have nourishment enough. Let the boy loose or I'll slice you from femoral to fang."

Jonathan stared at the creature in surprise. She was pretty, but not nearly as alluring as she had been a moment before. The mist about her had all but disappeared and he could see the bed of dirt on which she sat, surrounded by animal carcasses. His stomach rolled at the sight, and he grew appalled that he had been so taken by her.

With a petulant sigh the once beautiful creature released her grip on Jonathan, who darted to Moira's side.

"How do you expect me to survive this trip?" Her question was a whining moan, somewhat blurred by her still-protruding fangs.

"It will only be a few days' time, provided you do not eat our navigator."

"I was only wanting a midnight snack. I would not have *drained* him."

"That was not the agreement with your master."

"Yes, well. He doesn't have to lie here in a crate full of dirt for days on end."

"You have plenty of food in there with you."

"Rotting animals with stale blood. The reek is positively awful. How would you like to be locked up in a box with dead things?"

"Now you have lost your roaming privileges."

"What roaming privileges? I'm not even allowed to leave the crate! I'm barely allowed to sit up and stretch my arms."

"Don't punish her on my account," Jonathan told

Moira, surprising even himself. Somehow he felt sorry for her.

"You would defend your attacker?"

"She was just hungry."

"Mr. Maritime, come here please," Moira called, stepping away from the boxed woman. Jonathan reluctantly joined her. "Has this creature addled your brain? You were almost bitten!"

"Well, I think any of us would resort to unpleasant deeds when trapped as such. She is a coherent creature. Have compassion. If you remember, we have been in similar situations."

"I asked you not to speak of such things," Moira nearly hissed.

"I only mean to make a point. No human should be treated so. I wouldn't wish that kind of captivity on my worst enemy."

"Just because it is sentient does *not* mean it is human," she replied, but it was clear she had seen Jonathan's point of view.

Moira turned back to the creature. "You may roam the cargo hold, as long as there are no other crew members about. However, if I hear of any attacks, or if I discover any of my crew with so much as a scratch on them, you *will* be jettisoned from my ship. I do not care if we're in the middle of the Bermuda Triangle. Understood?"

"I don't think your benefactor would appreciate that."

"I said, *do you understand me?*"

"Yes," the dark haired woman grudgingly replied.

"Yes, what?"

"Yes, captain." Her response was a low, animal-like, hiss that sent chills down Jonathan's spine. How he had thought her human, he could not fathom. Her eyes seemed to glow in the half-light, her skin was beyond pale—she was the shade of white reserved for bloodless corpses.

Satisfied with the creature's answer, Moira headed out.

Not waiting for an invitation, Jonathan hurried up the stairs after her.

"What is that creature?" he asked, stopping her at the entrance to the galley.

"A sanguine beast. It feeds off humans."

"Why is it aboard this ship?"

"These creatures are sensitive to the light of day. To travel long distances, they must be kept in a dark place. We have been charged with seeing it reaches its destination."

"Have you transported other such creatures?"

"Yes."

"While I have been aboard?" he asked, not entirely sure he wished to know the answer.

"Yes," Moira replied, her face hard and devoid of emotion.

"And you do not feel the need to warn the crew of such potentially dangerous creatures?"

Moira sighed deeply. "How do you think a lot of superstitious sailors would react to monsters in the hold? It is bad enough my being a woman; I'm already a token of bad luck to many."

Jonathan wanted to argue, but he understood her position. It was a difficult situation to be in. Yet it still seemed strange and wrong.

"I see what you are saying," he replied and she turned on her heel to leave. "One more question, if I may!" he called. She turned back, impatient and ready to be rid of his presence. "Who is this benefactor we make all these deliveries for?"

Moira bowed her head a little. "I think…that is a conversation for another day."

Jonathan watched as she walked up the stairs and out of sight.

Considering the frightening cargo, he again wondered if he really wanted to learn the answers to his own questions.

~~~~

The water-logged bit of crate peeled away until just a few pulpy flakes remained. These too, soon wavered into nonexistence.

The smoke cleared from Banon's eye as he turned to look at his brothers.

"How have we not heard of your crew's interactions with the supernatural?" Angus asked.

"We see much, but very few of us ever leave the ship to spread tales," Banon told them.

"Where did you say these events occurred?" Killian asked.

Banon smirked. "I didn't."

"Is it a big secret?" Patrick laughed slightly.

"No, not at all. They occurred here," Banon replied to their surprise.

"*Here*?" Patrick asked.

"These are old stories by Vacant Realm standards," Banon replied. "You don't remember when I used to sail here?"

"I do," Angus muttered.

"It was a rebellious time for me." Banon continued. "Who knew it would lead to my life's calling?"

"Where you hardly watch your own land," Angus challenged.

"I am rarely needed down there," Banon scoffed. "Besides, their cities are so spread out I can better serve by being mobile. Anyway, these stories took place right before the gods were banished."

"Oh yes, I remember. That was when Olympus became Gods' Grace," Killian replied.

"It was growing a bit crowded here," Angus groaned. "And don't get me started on the cult of the one true god."

"Oh yes, the Masons." Banon nodded, thinking on the bad memories.

"They have many names, and many factions," Killian commented. "Anyway, this land had two more witchdoctors than needed."

"Yes well, now that you have Gods' Grace, Killian, it has been quite manageable." Angus sighed.

"I've always been curious," Patrick interrupted. "How do you travel so easily between the worlds, Banon? Especially the Vacant Realm. I nearly end up in the Arctic every time I come here."

"Well, we do not make the trip often," Banon confessed. "Our benefactor makes the transition easier."

"The Bermuda Triangle is not an *easy* path, even with the appropriate magic," Killian commented. "You should not be so blasé about it."

"I'm not. We just have a…less difficult way. A back door of sorts." Banon smirked.

"This is all fascinating, Banon, but perhaps we should let someone else have the floor," Angus called. "Killian, perhaps you have another to share?"

"I have one last tale," he told them and removed a long, thin object from his pocket. "I offer this tale of a dismal life doomed to end in bloodshed," he announced as he placed it upon the table where it sprang to life becoming a small creature that slithered and flopped in a disoriented circle.

THE LOVE OF MEDUSA

People had once flocked from all over Greece to see the magnificent Temple of Athena. The temple had lain in a virtual paradise, that is until Athena razed the island and its inhabitants to utter oblivion. Now, the island lay barren, the trees leafless—naught but a forest of skeletal silhouettes starkly etched by the setting sun.

Ancient abandoned vessels lined the tiny coast, marking the waters where they rose to the shallow's edge. The ships, once the pride of their various regions, floated desolate and dead, nothing more than additions to a cryptic collection, much as their masters to Medusa's ever-expanding Stone Garden.

Medusa slithered across the deserted ruins which served as her prison. Squinting against the sun, she gazed down at the shore, recalling the island's former glory. Lately, the threat of a new ship on the horizon seemed ever-present. The one now was just a speck in the distance. Soon enough it would breach her shore and a new horde would disembark, in search of her head.

Medusa picked at the statue of her latest victim. He wasn't much older than she had been when cursed to this wretched existence. She longed to trade places—he was free to run in the Elysian Fields, eternally happy. She, on the other hand, was cursed with immortality. True, on a few occasions, she had been close to death; yet each time, when she thought release would finally be hers, Hades—eyes averted from her petrifying gaze—sent her away. She could die, she could be slain, but Athena's curse kept her soul rooted to her serpentine body. The afterlife was forever out of her reach.

There were no Elysian Fields for monsters.

Gingerly, Medusa touched the fresh scar on her cheek. The last ship to visit had brought Spartans onto her shore—brave soldiers come to conquer the mighty snake-haired Gorgon, vicious and vile men, the lot of them. If not for her cursed stare, they might have gotten her. In the end however, victory had been hers. Another fleet turned to stone. Trinkets for her Gothic gallery of failed heroes.

The great screeching of her sisters drew Medusa's attention to the sea. They cried warnings of the oncoming ship, which advanced faster than expected. Why her sisters cared whether she lived or died, Medusa did not know. Even they, her own blood, could not meet her deadly gaze. They kept their distance, protecting her from afar.

Medusa did not know of her monstrous sisters until after she had been cursed. Nor did she know her parents were great sea creatures. In hindsight, this lineage made sense. The priestesses of the temple had raised her. However, she had always been drawn to the sea. Perhaps that was why *he* had taken an interest in the first place.

Her former life seemed a pleasant dream. So many years had passed on this desolate island. Had her face ever been framed by golden locks instead of hissing snakes? Had she ever danced on white sand shores with adoring patrons? Had she ever been surrounded by anything but death? Her old life seemed so silly compared to this harsh reality; yet she would give anything to have it back.

Tonight was the full moon. Her one night of peace every cycle—the night the sea was at its most beautiful.

As she made her way across the vast temple, Medusa found her reflection in a shard of mirror. She could just make out her face: still young, still cruelly beautiful despite the scars and snakes of her hair. It was an evil joke that her face had not changed— Athena's constant reminder of what Medusa had once been, of her former humanity. Without this face it would be almost easy to forget she was ever raised as a human, so easy to be lost beneath the snakes and claws and scales.

The serpents crowning her head curled around her face, as if to comfort her. It was painful even for Medusa to look into her own eyes. They seemed every color at once. It made her temples ache, yet it was difficult to look away. She suspected this was how the warriors felt: compelled to look into the eyes of death, to peek into Pandora's Box.

Medusa slithered solemnly toward the back gardens of the demolished temple. There thrived the only life left on the miserable island. There she surveyed the beautiful grounds fed by the waters of a spring fountain. This place, the only bit of island left untouched by Athena's wrath, was her sanctuary. The garden was a gift from her beloved, a place teeming with flora and light. Here, there were no eyes to see her, no flesh to turn to stone. Flowers of every kind grew—their colors so vivid, so full of life. It was the one place Medusa felt a connection to her former self.

At the edge of the fountain Medusa coiled and waited, watching the shifting colors of the sky as the sun sank beneath the sea. Finally, the moon rose in its brilliance causing the ocean to sparkle. She sat, entranced by this beauty while behind her the waters of the fountain stirred.

The spring rose, gently frothed, and shifted as a flowing form emerged. Strong, wet arms wrapped around her shoulders. With a sigh, she settled back into their embrace.

"How are you this evening, dearest?" a strong voice echoed.

Her heart leaped. Gently hissing, the snakes of her hair calmed, her eyes closed, and she smiled. "Better now."

The fluid figure rose up to sit next to her on the fountain's ledge. She gazed at the translucent liquid version of the man with whom she'd fallen in love so many years ago. His cool lips brushed hers, his waters calmly washing over them. He tenderly returned her gaze.

And winced.

Even in this form, her eyes had the power to bring him pain. Medusa's heart sank; she could see the hurt reflected in the pools of his eyes. She quickly looked back out to the sea.

"It is beautiful, isn't it?" he asked her.

"You know it is." She laughed lightly.

"It's all for you." His cool hands ran down her arms, sending shivers through her. "Sing for me."

"No, my love," she replied solemnly. "My voice has gone to rust with misuse. I have no time for such frivolity. Warriors come by the dozens to cut me down."

"Your voice is sweet as ever." He sighed, kissing her cheek. There he noticed the fresh scar. "They have marred your beautiful face."

"You are a fool to call me beautiful," she hissed sadly. "These hunters, they grow in number and strength. Or perhaps I grow tired. I have been here too long."

"I have pleaded with Zeus to free you. However—"

"I am a danger. He will not let me go. No living thing can survive my gaze—not even you."

Medusa continued to watch the approaching ship. There was nothing he or anyone could do to stop this newest onslaught. Athena decreed anyone looking for Medusa's head would find calm waters and a favorable wind between their ship and the island. Her love had argued with Zeus, but Athena would not be reasoned with—not even by the king of the gods.

"They are coming for you, my dearest," he told her suddenly.

She wasn't surprised. He always tried to warn her when danger was nigh, but never so bluntly. "I saw the ship on the horizon this morning," she told him, staring at the daunting silhouette in the distance.

This one made her uneasy; there was something different about it. In all her years she had never seen a faster ship. "Let them come," Medusa told him with false confidence, "I will be ready."

"Not this time," he replied, to her surprise. "He is a son of Zeus."

Medusa looked to the flowers of her garden. She had lived here so long, wishing she could leave, wishing she could put an end to this gruesome imprisonment. Now her love said she would soon be conquered.

"You can try to fight him, but he will win," he told her sadly.

"You wish me not to fight? You *want* him to take my head?"

"I want nothing of the sort. But there is nothing you can do." She could feel his grief. "Athena has shown him how to defeat you."

Medusa sat silently. Many times she had longed to die, longed for the afterlife, whatever it held for her. Now, hearing she would be dead upon the ship's arrival, she was not sure what she wanted.

"Then let me die." Medusa sighed. "Perhaps I will finally find my peace in the Underworld."

"Athena will not let you go so easily."

"Easy?" Her snakes hissed and recoiled. "You call centuries of entrapment on this island, of being tangled in this body, *easy*?"

"Steady, my love," he soothed. "Athena has decreed you *will* be defeated. But she has bound you in this body, and so you will remain. Zeus's son wants your head to defeat the kraken, and Athena wants it as a trophy. There you will be captive. Forever looking out from her shield."

"Dreadful!" Medusa hissed. "This is to be my fate?"

"I have a solution," he replied. "I cannot keep him from slaying you. However, I can keep you from an eternity of service to Athena."

"How?" she asked, her snakes' tongues flickering. All their eyes turned towards him.

"*Sleep*, my love. Morpheus will keep you in dreams until Athena has done with you. You will not wake. You will not feel the blade. Nor any other torment."

Medusa rested against him once more, his rippling waters soothing her angst. She only ever felt at peace when she slept, when the sighing and susurrations of the snakes were finally silent, a far more agreeable fate than the alternative.

"Then I am to remain that way forever?" she asked.

"Faith, my love. I will come for you, as I have come every waxing moon." He smiled down at her, softly placing his cool, damp cheek against hers. "Until then, be steady. Sing for me. Sing, and think of what sweet dreams await you in Morpheus's care."

Poseidon wrapped his aqueous arms around her. Enveloped in the lapping tranquility of his embrace, Medusa sang sweet songs of water nymphs and sea creatures. Her voice was rough, but her songs could still tempt the gods down from Olympus.

She and Poseidon lay together by the fountain until the sun rose. There she remained when Zeus's son claimed her head.

~~~~

The slithering snake of a creature had shrunk in size, having shed several layers. It circled amongst its dead skins until its final layer peeled away into nothing and disintegrated.

"A sad ending, Brother," Patrick called.

"Sad to some," Killian replied. "Others would see it as an escape from a terrible existence."

As one, the brothers turned to the door, alarmed by a sudden clamoring above.

"Thank the gods," Angus sighed in relief. "Conner's finally arrived."

"I had no doubt he would." Banon chuckled, rolling

his eyes at Angus. "Told you he would never miss a ball."

The door to the great room came open with sudden force then.

"This land possesses the most fascinating motorized vehicles. So many of them!" Conner sighed as he tripped into the room, a bit of twisting ivy from the front yard still fighting to ensnare him. "They roam about on smooth roads, not dirt or cobblestone. Such differences since last I was here. They're not powered by steam anymore and some hardly use gas! Who would've thought!"

"You forgot the bypass spell for the front yard, didn't you?" Angus asked his newly arrived and very distracted brother.

"I cannot be expected to remember every little thing! I haven't been to your place in a hundred years. Not that I don't love you, dear brother, but I much prefer the hotels set up for the ball. So many interesting creatures to bump into in the halls. Oh, and the after-parties!" He stopped then, looked around at his brothers, and adjusted his worn top hat which was adorned with beaten brass goggles that rested snugly on the brim. "Am I late?"

"*Late*? We only have a few hours left to sunrise," Angus replied tersely. "We were beginning to think you weren't going to show."

Conner checked the great leather and brass watch upon his wrist. "So sorry. This thing always gets thrown off by the transition." He struck the face in annoyance, causing the hands to spin a few times in response.

"It might be simpler to learn to read the clocks here, youngest Brother."

"That is not fair, *eldest Brother*," Conner shot back, annoyed." I cannot tell the difference between a clock and a thermometer here, there are too many variations. In my land, a clock has a face, a thermometer is a thin mercury tube, and we operate by the numerals."

"Roman numerals," Angus corrected.

"We were using numerals long before your *Romans*."

"Brothers," Killian interrupted, "We are running out of time! Perhaps this conversation can wait until we've finished our offerings."

"Yes, why don't you share your offering, Conner," Angus announced.

"Well, I wasn't prepared to present so quickly, but alright." He pulled a small pocket watch from the vest under his long coat. "Now let me see here." He sat up a little straighter and then cleared his throat. "I offer this tale of a brilliant young techromancer—my apprentice—and his first steps out of a life of crime and into a great adventure. I sacrifice this pocket watch which once belonged to him but was replaced by a more efficient model."

Conner then placed the pocket watch upon the table where it, like all the metal-based trinkets before it, began to rust and tarnish.

RHETT STEAMRUN

The night was filled with fog so thick one could hardly see a hand in front of their face, let alone a gang of boys lurking across an alleyway. This particular passage was especially dim—one of the few in the Industrial Domain still lit with gas lamps instead of electric lights.

Everett waited patiently for their target to reach the flickering street lamp on the corner. That's when he'd give Glasser the signal.

His nights were often spent in this fashion: scouting wealthy areas for the boys to pickpocket. It was their way of life. But lately it had become tiresome. It wasn't that Everett had suddenly developed a fresh moral outlook on stealing. The rich hoarded their wealth and could afford to lose a few coins—*especially* in the Industrial Domain. Industrialites spent ridiculous amounts on trinkets and baubles designed to assist with tedious tasks like brushing teeth and knotting gold-embossed bow ties. Everett heard there was now a machine designed to tie shoes! Citizens of the Industrial Domain had actually grown too lazy to bend over their own stuffed bellies. What was this bloody world coming to?

Checking the pocket-watch in his waistcoat, he felt twitchy. He always felt this way before something bad happened. Tonight, he had an idea of where that bad feeling may be coming.

Glasser.

Normally, he and his brethren kept a low profile when thieving. They only targeted those who looked as though they could afford it. No more than a couple targets a week, and *never* in the same spot. Ignoring these rules was exactly how people got caught, and Glasser was growing dangerously close to overstepping that line.

The fool had been pushing high-end hits in the same wealthy areas, night after night. The others said nothing because of the payout. The upstart had even roughed up the last couple of targets, leaving them with black eyes, a broken arm in one case. There had been a small blurb about it in the back of the local paper, *Industrial Highlights*. The boys weren't exactly making headlines, but they *were* garnering attention, which was both foolhardy and dangerous.

Ever since hitting puberty, Glasser had been reckless. Their patriarch, Varlet, had warned them about the powerful effects of hormones. He'd said the onset of manhood was a delicate time in which it was the most important—and the most difficult—to keep a level head. Glasser was *not* adjusting well to this transition. Then again, the boy rarely listened. Everett was only sixteen himself, but he heeded his lessons and learned fast, faster than the other boys. And definitely faster than Glasser.

The flash of an emerald necklace caught his eye, pulling him back to the here and now. Their target had finally reached the hissing lamppost. Everett pulled a flint lighter from his vest and flicked it once as the target turned onto the side street. Almost instantly, his four companions, headed by Glasser, hurried into the alley, hot on the lightly clicking heels of the lady's shiny designer shoes.

Everett never felt bad for stealing, not when the choice was between a new necklace for an air-headed Industrialite or a meal for him. But he had never relished the taste of harming others. However, theft kept him fed, healthy, and even funded his experiments. Experiments sure to make him rich, boosting him to a whole new level of thievery where people would happily hand him their money, rather than Everett happily handing himself their money. That's all business is, really: stealing the honest way.

Everett waited a moment, making sure the street

was deserted, and followed the boys into the sideway. He could faintly hear the woman struggling as he approached.

"We got it," one of the boys called as they rushed past with the necklace. "Best hurry back to the Boiler Room, it's getting late."

"What about Glasser and Hodge?" Everett asked.

"Said they'd meet us. Don't worry, *we* got the jewels," the other boy insisted as they hurried into the fog.

Everett moved to follow when he heard muffled screaming from the passage behind him. Were Hodge and Glasser still holding the girl? What where they up to now? Cautiously, Everett stepped back against the heavily shadowed wall and crept forward. When his eyes finally adjusted to the dim alleyway, he spotted three figures in the mist. Something was wrong.

"Hurry up then," Hodge whined impatiently. "How many more valuables could she possibly have?"

"Quite a few." Glasser's chuckle was low and dark. "Why don't you run along? She won't put up a fight. Will you, dearie."

"You never leave a brother without back up. Rule number one," Hodge insisted.

"Just go!"

"If you get into trouble, Varlet'll take it out on me."

"Do it! And if I find you've told anyone, I'll have your head on a pike," Glasser threatened.

Without another word Hodge ran off, passing Everett without so much as a blink of an eye.

Silently, Everett approached Glasser and the target.

When he finally reached them, anger flamed red in his cheeks. It was now clear exactly *which* valuables Glasser was after—the degenerate was fussing with the lady's skirts. Everett could put up with the attitude, even the violent tantrums, but this was the last straw. *Someone* had to teach Glasser a lesson.

Unhitching a leather case at the side of his belt, he turned a small crank within, thus initiating the chain reaction. He only ever used his defense mechanism in emergencies, but Glasser was spry. Who knew what he would do when confronted. A gentle humming—taut with unseen energy—coursed through the line that ran up Everett's back, over his left shoulder, and down to his hand.

His steps were careful as he approached the struggling pair; one wrong move and the blade Glasser had at the girl's throat might slip.

Everett knew he would get the drop. Glasser was too busy getting tangled in her petticoats. Everett was suddenly glad it was fashionable for Industrialite women to wear so many flouncy layers.

In an instant, he snatched Glasser's dagger and placed a hand to the heathen's neck. The bright electric current dropped Glasser to the ground before he could utter a word.

"Run," Everett told the girl. Mute with shock, she gathered herself and hurried down the way, finding her voice to wail for the police once she reached the open street.

Glasser lay on the cobblestones struggling to regain the use of his muscles. Everett would have to adjust the power next time—the scoundrel was already coming around.

"What'd ya do that for?" he muttered, his words fuzzy as his lips proved uncooperative.

"You went too far this time, mate."

Everett dragged Glasser to the nearest gas lamp, removed a thick wire from his belt, and bound him to the post.

"Let me free and I'll let you continue breathing," Glasser hissed, clumsily struggling against him.

"I don't think so. You've broken too many rules. You're a danger, not just to me but to the rest of the boys," Everett cursed him.

"Your stupid tricks won't keep me here long," Glasser warned.

"Long enough. That wire is tested up to three hundred pounds. You aren't even a buck fifty."

"I'll tell Varlet. You don't turn on a *brother*."

"You aren't my brother." Everett glared at him. "You've gotten your way too long and now it's time to pay the piper. Maybe some time in lock-up will teach you how to behave. Good luck ratting me out from a jail cell."

"*Jail?*" Sirens sounded and hurried footsteps echoed down the alley next to them. "Let me go!" Glasser panicked. "I'll pay you anything. I have a stash under the loose boards beneath my mattress. You can have half!"

"Give the boys in stripes my regards." Everett smirked.

"You're no better than me, Steamrun! You're no

better!" The yells faded as Everett hurried out the side road, down a few narrow passageways, and finally out to the docks. The pickpocket knew his moral compass didn't exactly point north, but he couldn't stomach the abuse of innocents, no matter how spoiled and petulant they may be.

Everett sat at the air dock, his satchel close at his side. Glasser had a lot more stashed under the floorboards than he'd thought possible. The boy must have been cheating Varlet for *years*. It would be more than enough for a new start. He would have to change his name. Glasser wouldn't be locked up forever and Everett knew enough of the louse to know he was not the forgiving type.

A sister at the orphanage he'd been raised in used to call him 'Rhett.' Perhaps it was time for Everett's story to end and Rhett's story to begin.

~~~~

The mist cleared from Conner's eyes as he stared down at the twisted diminishing hunk of metal before him. "Pity, that was such a nice antique," he sighed as the exposed gears and springs of the watch tarnished, separated, and skittered across the great table into nothing.

"Your apprentice sounds like a handful." Patrick laughed.

"He is, but it is fascinating what he can do with

machinery. A true savant."

"We have two more tales to tell," Angus called, interrupting Conner's boasting. "Banon's last offering and my own."

"By all means, Brother, you first," Banon offered. "Your tales are always so serious. I would hate to have this meeting end on a down note."

"I am not sure how to take that, so I will just go ahead and share my final tale."

"Yes, let's do get on with this, I need to shop for a few last touches to my outfit for the ball," Conner commented excitedly.

"The stores are closed now," Angus replied.

"What I need I can certainly find at the all-hours corner markets," Conner replied clapping his hands together slightly in excitement. "I so love those."

With a roll of his eyes, Angus pulled a small chunk of rock from his pocket. It was almost a pebble and was black as night. "I offer this ancient tale of a creature so long lived that his origin lies with that of our world, long before unstable magics tore apart the thirteen lands. I sacrifice this piece of his being."

Angus placed the small rock upon the table where it smoldered, creating small flowing crevasses of red-hot magma which crept their way around the rock like exposed veins.

THE WRAITH

The crunching of dried leaves underfoot was rhythmic, slow, and relaxed. His target was unaware of being watched. This was going to be an easy kill; so easy it hardly seemed worth it, but the money was right.

The Wraith waited with rapidly diminishing patience and realized his mid-afternoon whiskey was wearing off. He checked his bag for another flask. No luck. Cursing his tolerance, the scruffy predator leaned against a thick branch and waited. His vantage point in the tree provided excellent camouflage and an easy view of his mark.

Slowly filling his lungs, he closed his eyes and listened. There was a lot to be learned by simply *listening*. He could tell if someone was careless or cunning, if someone had a limp or a hunched back, even the very mood they were in, if he only listened hard enough. The man, if he could still be classified as such, could hear *everything*. Not just the chirping of birds and the scurrying of marmots in the foliage. He could hear wolves stalking deer in the distance, fish splashing in the stream a mile away, even the whispered creaking of the trees. It was easy for him, no more strenuous than breathing. *Ignoring* it was the difficult part. If he hadn't learned to drown out the damnable cacophony years ago, he might have gone mad. He could hear every creature in a five-mile radius, but not one of them could hear him. It was vital he stay calm while tracking and hunting; if his emotions flared they would sense him, as sure as they could sense a forest fire.

He groaned as he listened to the man's steps: his prey was in no hurry and would not be in striking distance for some time. With little else to do, he took his knife and began flaying an apple, red from white. He hated waiting.

Idleness was his greatest enemy, static moments tempted bad memories, memories of death, cities in ruin, rivers of blood, lovers engulfed in flame. They were all visions of another life—of a man formerly known as McTrave. He had been a good man, a man operating by the codes of honor and valor, a king among men. That man would be disgusted by what he saw now: a two-bit assassin for hire known simply as the Wraith. It was a name given to him by those who had survived his brief company. He was a horrifying apparition moving through the world. *McTrave* had died long ago, shriveled and disappeared after seeing everything he cared for reduced to ashes.

After spending years hunting ghosts, the man had given up. The old McTrave thought he could find a way to bring her back, but he'd traveled from one end of Ithiria to the other and—nothing. Each devil he encountered was naught but a waste of time. Any mystic worth their salt knew better than to consort with him; they could sense what he was. They knew to be in his presence was to tempt death. Years had passed and McTrave was no closer to getting her back than he was to finding a way to rid himself of this cursed existence. He was no more than nightmares in a fearsome shell.

With nothing left to live for, McTrave had set to wandering, taking jobs where he could, simply to afford the drink, and doing the one thing at which he excelled: destroying life. He took no joy in his endeavors and was sure to be quick in closing deals. No need to cause the slaughtered more suffering than necessary.

His exploits had become legend. The terrible deeds were even used to frighten children away from the woods. Well, at least he'd achieved some good, he thought as he tossed his apple core, pulled a rolled cigar from his bag, and lit it with the spontaneous flick of a finger. What did he care if he was reduced to a story-book monster? Even the followers of The One True God were starting to adopt his misdeeds into their lore. How he hated the pious contradictions of this new religion. He'd spent years setting fire to their temples, but every time he destroyed one, two more sprung up in its place like some terrible hydra.

The bastards.

The Wraith took one long drag of his cigar, instantly reducing it to ash. Annoyed, he sent the burnt remnants fluttering to the ground, yet another cigar ruined by his infernal temper.

He leaned back, trying to get his mind in the game, and heard footsteps approach. To work, he thought as he cleaned the blade of his hunting knife. He waited as the target leisurely passed beneath his hiding place in the foliage. The man was actually whistling. So jolly, so carefree. For a moment, the Wraith almost hated to strike, but he was in the perfect position. It was keep it clean now or let it get messy later.

With a step, the Wraith plummeted to the forest floor and in an instant it was done. His prey continued a pace before realizing anything was wrong. Curiously, he wiped the blood from his throat and looked at his hand. He turned to the Wraith questioningly, then gurgled as he fell to the forest floor.

"There are worse deaths," he told the dead man as though it might be some comfort to his corpse.

Just then, McTrave caught a draft on the wind. He smelled something familiar, something he had smelled on the man who hired him. Glaring down, the Wraith used a foot to roll the body onto its back. The *man*, his prey, was no more than a boy, his facial hair just starting to grow. He couldn't be older than sixteen. What could a boy of his age have done to deserve death?

Then, he realized what he was seeing: the hair, the eyes. They were identical to his client's. It wasn't until then that he understood what he had been paid to do. He was accustomed to dealing with murderers, cheating husbands, thieving employees, revenge, an eye for an eye, the whole bit—but not this. Why hadn't he noticed before? He steadied himself on the trunk of a tree. What did he care that he had been paid to kill the man's own son? Why should that bother him?

It was the boy. He had been so happy, so unsuspecting, no idea his own blood wanted him dead. The Wraith didn't kill children, despite popular belief. True, he was a monster, but even he had his limitations.

"His father would only have hired someone else," came a creaky voice from behind him.

He didn't need to turn to know who, or rather *what*, was there. "I should have asked. I know better than to go into a job blind," he replied, staring bitterly at the dead boy.

Had he grown so tired of it all that he could let something like this slip?

"You're burning it," the voice called.

The Wraith looked up to the smoldering hand print he'd made in the tree.

"Malachi, we need to speak," the voice, little more

than the crackling of burning leaves and smoldering wood, groaned.

"Do not call me that. I am *not* Malachi."

The Wraith pulled his hand from the burning bark, cleaned the boy's blood from his knife, and turned to the thing behind him. The little creature was more rock than man: a three-foot hunk of smoldering volcanic magma with stubby appendages and the vague suggestion of facial features.

"We have nothing to discuss. Now go away." His growl was both demanding and pleading.

"No, Malachi," it replied. "This time *you* must hear me. Things are happening, things you will be part of."

"Why? Why can't you find someone else?" The creature of fire had followed him since he could remember, but it had always left when commanded, without question. Why the hell wouldn't it leave now?

"There is no one else," the little creature replied. "This is not the existence you wish. Why pursue what you hate?"

"This is all that is left of me," the Wraith muttered.

The creature looked saddened but did not back down. "I will help you, I know what plagues you. I see it. I feel it."

"You do not know my pain!" the Wraith hissed, the leaves beneath his feet smoldering.

"Not as you do, no. I see you are tormented. I know you do not want others to suffer."

The Wraith did not argue.

"Follow me," the creature said. "I will hide the memories, but that is the limit of my ability."

The Wraith looked at him fully for the first time. "You can make them go away?"

The little creature hesitated. "It is dangerous. I cannot block one memory alone. I can take all, or nothing. Eventually the effect will wane. When it does, there is no telling what will happen, but it will be painful."

"I do not care," he replied darkly. "Anything is better than this torment."

The little creature sighed heavily. "As you wish."

"What do you need me to do?" His eyes blazed.

"You must guard an item vital to the existence of this world. I will show you."

The creature started into the woods, moving faster than its stature should allow.

The Wraith followed. He did not want his memories, any of them. He did not care for this life and would do anything to be rid of his past. It seemed amazing that the little creature of fire had been the key to his salvation all along. He knew the creature would not have agreed had it not been desperate for his help, but the Wraith did not care, no matter the danger. If McTrave could not find her, could not die to join her, then the Wraith must forget her. If that meant forgetting everything, so be it.

~~~~

The smoldering pebble was now but a small pile of liquid magma. As it sank into the table it left a reddish mar upon the wood, one that did not entirely disappear. Angus touched the spot but quickly pulled his hand away. Much too hot to touch.

"Is that normal?" Patrick asked.

"Normal? No," Angus replied. "Should I have expected it? Yes. This tree is old, connected to the very core of Ithiria. That rock was a fragment of the fire and chaos elements. I should have expected it would leave a mark."

"Will it go away?"

"I don't know, but let me worry about that later. We have one last tale to tell and then we can start our preparations for the ball. Banon, your last story if you will."

"Sure," he replied as he pulled a black barnacle from his pocket. He placed it upon the table to begin his story when the barnacle all but caught fire with a burst of dark energy.

The brothers' spines straightened—shoulders and backs taut and rigid, their eyes filled with black and snapped towards the heart of the tree. Suddenly, the blackness in their eyes sparked a bright green. A swirling vortex emanated from the tree, circling the room before encompassing the brothers entirely.

MCBANE

As usual, Moira woke before the sun had even the slightest inclination to rise. She had always been an early riser. This had been a positive attribute aboard the *Persephone*, but thanks to her new shipmates, the habit had become more of an annoyance.

The captain silently cursed her new charges. It was madness to force the entire crew to sail at night and sleep during the day for the sake of a passenger. Unfortunately, this decision was beyond her control—as was the direction in which they headed. The

Arabian Desert was an unpleasant land awash with pirates, like themselves, but she did not much care for their dealings or demeanor.

What use was being captain if Moira could not control the destination of her own ship, or even the times in which it operated? She had become a hired hand to the underworld, and though she was grateful for the favors she'd been granted, the cost had proven to be quite high.

It had been a while since their benefactor, who insisted on being referred to as such, had called upon them. She should have known the lull was too good to be true. Contacting her out of the blue, he had demanded she and her crew immediately assist some wayward adventures. And at the Ithirian conference too, what timing. How could he possibly think she and her crew could be prepared for such a venture?

Still unable to sleep, Moira made her way to the deck. It was a beautiful day, the sea sparkled brightly and not a single cloud marred the sky. At this time, the deck should have been awash with sailors, readying for the day's voyage. Now it was practically a ghost ship. Only the day-watch lingered, half asleep from trying to rest during a night of rowdy announcements.

It was dangerous to have the crew sleep during the day. True, some pirates attacked at night, but most battles took place in the daylight hours. And while they were renowned in the pirating world, there were still those who either sought to hunt the *Persephone* or didn't know any better. The last thing she needed was some amateur getting a lucky strike and losing half her cargo because her crew was asleep at the helm. That was one aspect on which their benefactor showed no leniency. No cargo was ever to be lost; if it was, they *must* go to any means to retrieve it. A happening she vowed never to encounter again.

Moira felt slightly more at ease now that she was looking out on the ocean. She had seen many strange things in her life, but no matter where she went, the ocean was the same, as constant and unchanging as the sky. This offered her a simple comfort. The sea could be a brutal mistress, but if you abided her laws, she would take you to the ends of the world, absolute freedom.

With a sigh, Moira headed back to her cabin. She was nearly at the door when she heard a ruckus below deck.

The clanging continued as Moira descended the stair into the galley. There, to her surprise, she found the very charge she had just been cursing.

The girl crouched, struggling to pick up a slew of metal pots and dishes scattered across the floor. As far as vampires went, this was the strangest Moira had ever come across. She was pale, as most were, but her hair was so black it almost seemed no color at all. Her eyes, likewise, were so dark they appeared as two voids in a porcelain mask. Looking into them was like looking into the depths of Tartarus. She very much reminded Moira of their benefactor in that respect.

The *Persephone* had transported zombies, mummies, even werewolves. But vampires were her least favorite. Being that one of their benefactor's favors was eternal life, they did not have to worry much about passengers killing crew; however, that protection did not expand to virus immunity. More than once a supernatural passenger had insisted on treating one of the crew as a midnight snack. Now Moira had several infected crew members, ranging from vampires to were-men, of both land and sea varieties. She was beyond exasperation.

The girl looked up at her in surprise. "I'm sorry, I'll clean it up."

"What are you doing down here?" Moira enquired. "It is almost daylight and I'm to understand your people have a strong aversion to the sun."

"Midnight snack," she replied continuing to fuss with the pots.

"Let the steward do it," Moira replied as the girl awkwardly stacked the toppled pots.

"And have him hate me forever?" she scoffed. "The last person I'd want to piss off on this ship is the one who controls the food."

"Fair enough," Moira replied dryly. "Just place them in the wash tub. You'll wake the rest of the crew if you continue with this banging about. They are having a hard enough time keeping this schedule."

"Oh, yeah." The girl bowed her head a little. Did she actually feel bad about putting them out? "You know, you don't have to do that for me."

"I am doing it because our benefactor wishes it."

The benefactor had promised there would be no more passenger details. Now, here she was, leading yet another voyage of the damned to who knows where. He insisted this was somehow different. Moira did not see how. She was still stuck with a new vampire and several other undead creatures—who were at this moment napping in the hold.

Moira much preferred cargo runs. They were simply required to pick up an item in one destination and drop it off in another. However, being forced to ferry passengers was irritating at best. Hardly a single one of them had any sea experience, and they always required some sort of special accommodation or dietary need. And now, not only did the *Persephone* have to transport passengers, she and her crew were expected to escort them around while turning the entire ship upside down to accommodate their exotic demands.

Even worse, instead of a simple week-long endeavor, they were on the hunt for something, and Moira would be stuck carting these creatures around until they found it—a task she was whole-heartedly committed to. The sooner they found what they were searching for, the sooner they would be off her ship.

"Benefactor?" the vampire girl asked. Then her eyes went wide in realization. "Oh, right. Well, I could try to speak to him about it. I don't mind if people work during the day."

"He is not in the habit of listening to anyone. Why would he listen to you?" Moira asked suspiciously.

"Uh, never mind that, but if you did want to switch back, it's alright by me."

"I was under the impression you and your kind slept during these hours," Moira continued, hoping to inspire the girl to return to her cabin.

"Usually, yeah. But I can't sleep. All this rocking makes me queasy."

"Some find it soothing."

"Well I am clearly not one of those." She laughed. "You got anything to eat around here?"

Moira stood perturbed; she would have to speak to their new second who had clearly neglected to show the girl where her food was kept. "I believe your *provisions* are located in a cold storage near your cabin," Moira replied, surprised the vampire hadn't smelled out the blood.

"No, no, I mean real food," she replied.

Moira paused, staring at the vampire curiously. "Am I to understand you would like some…human food?"

"Yes, Red Vines if you got 'em."

Moira stood at a loss. She had never encountered anything as strange as this creature. "We have a cupboard just there." She pointed to an old, wooden cupboard which somewhat resembled an ice box. "Think of what it is you wish to eat and it will accommodate you."

The vampire gave Moira a crooked look and went to the door where she took the handle and said aloud, "Red Vines."

"There is no need to speak to it, the apparatus senses your desire," she corrected, but the girl just looked even more confused and opened the cupboard.

"Hells yeah!" the vampire cried, pulling a little plastic-wrapped package of red candy ropes from the cupboard. Moira turned to leave as the girl tore open the package and began gnawing happily on a piece of rope. "Hey, so when is this love boat going to port?"

"When we reach our destination," Moira replied, pausing at the stair.

"Which is when?"

"A month's time."

"A *m-month*?" the girl stammered. "No shore leave, or whatever you call it, for that long?"

"As you can see we are well-stocked. No need to make unnecessary detours."

"How about stopping for the sake of our sanity?"

"I am afraid looking after your sanity is not part of my job description. However, you may speak with our physician, Banon if you are having—mental issues," she replied, curiously staring at the girl as she ate the red ropes.

"I'm sorry, did you want one?" the vampire asked, offering one of the oddly shining ropes to Moira.

"No, I am quite alright. Eating before sleep does not agree with me."

"Oh yeah, my brother's the same way. He gets all 'ooh, brains' night of the living dead, ya know?"

"Not as such. I do hope you enjoy your snack and find the inspiration to rest. I will take my leave. Good day."

"Yeah, you too," the vampire replied, opening and re-shutting the food cupboard to collect more of the red colored vines.

Moira walked up the stairs, perplexed. The girl was strange, yet somehow amusing. So unlike the other *damned* creatures she had been charged to sail with.

Moira had a growing feeling this trip might not be like the others.

Just then she heard another loud clamoring from the galley. A chill ran up her spine and she forced herself to continue to her bed. Yes, this voyage may prove more interesting than any other. Unfortunately, interesting did not always mean good.

~~~~

The barnacle glowed with dark energy but did not dissipate as the other items had. It remained lit with the bright green energy as the swirling vortex emanating from the dark eye whipped at their hair and clothes. The miniature cyclone twisted in tighter and tighter until finally disappearing into the brothers entirely.

Slowly, the green of their eyes died away and the men sat rejuvenated. Their skin appeared brighter, their eyes alight, their hair fuller. Though energized, the brothers sat stunned and confused as Banon retrieved the black barnacle from the old tree.

"My story was rejected?" he muttered in confusion.

"What do you mean? Is that not what we just saw?" Conner asked.

'It had to be the story," Killian added. "We received the blessings."

"I know my story," Banon replied. "That was something else."

"It was the future," Angus sighed dismally. "Your story must have triggered it."

"I think you're right," Banon muttered, clearly unnerved. "That dark-haired vampire has never been aboard my ship."

"So, is it a vision from the Fates or the oak itself?" Killian asked seriously. "We have received its power once more."

"I would assume the oak," Angus sighed. "The Fates are strong but not strong enough to do more than interrupt our ritual. They could not bypass it altogether like this. Which means this is not something we can wait to let happen. This *must* happen."

"You say you know this girl?" Banon asked Angus. "What would she want aboard my ship?"

"I was to help her find someone. I had a vague idea of where he might be but was unsure how to get her there. Now I think the issue has been resolved."

Banon stared at him, stunned. "You do know I am not the captain of the ship. I cannot decide who does and does not board. Captain McBane has never taken kindly to carting around passengers. She will not be easily persuaded."

"Then I believe your benefactor might have some say in the matter, since we have seen it come to pass. You must speak with him at the ball."

"Me?" Banon sputtered. "What makes you think he will listen to anything I have to say? Killian, you seem to like him, you talk to him."

"I am not opposed to asking," Killian replied calmly.

"I have a feeling he will not protest in this matter," Angus told them.

"What makes you so sure?" Banon scoffed.

"Just a hunch," Angus replied, staring at the eye thoughtfully. "Well, it looks as though we have our work cut out for us. Shall we adjourn?"

"Agreed," Killian called as the others nodded in acceptance.

All stood and left the great oak table, filing into the long twisting earth walkway back to the front of Angus's strange home.

"Do any of you require a place to stay for the evening?" Angus asked as they came into the entry room.

"No, no. I couldn't think to intrude," Killian called. "I will go catch up with Ferdinand. The King offered me one of his rooms for the days of the ball. He arrives tomorrow."

"It will be nice to see life in these vacant homes again," Angus replied. "Conner? Are you sure I cannot offer you accommodations?"

"No, but who can sleep with the Ball around the corner?" Conner mused. "I have so much shopping and trading to do with the blanketed men of the streets."

"Blanketed men of the streets?" Angus inquired in confusion.

"Yes, the ones with the wire carts."

"The transients. I see. Well, this explains your last few formal outfits."

"And you, Banon? Ready for what's ahead?"

"I think we can manage one young girl." He chuckled. "My captain will be displeased, but she often is when matters are out of her hands."

"Are you truly interested in traveling?" Banon asked Patrick then.

"Oh, I have too many responsibilities to get lost with the likes of your crew." He laughed.

"I suppose not, but our former navigator has taken a captain's position in your Old World, running some learning programs across the lands," Banon informed him.

"The Extension Program?"

"Yes, I believe that's what he called it. You should join him. Jonathan could use someone to look out for him. They only spend a limited time in each land, so you wouldn't be gone too long, maybe even make some new contacts along the way. Besides, with taking on this girl I might not be able to get all the blessings to our brothers. Here, take some of them." Banon smiled, offering his hand.

Patrick thought a moment before accepting his hand. Their eyes momentarily lit with green as Banon passed on their shares of their covenant.

"You have a place to stay then?" Angus called after Banon.

"On my ship. I don't sleep well on land. As much as I would love to stay here and listen to rousing stories of your antique collecting, I have a new navigator to drink under the deck."

"Go on then," Angus replied, trying to hide a smirk. "I'll see you at the Ball tomorrow. Try not to be too hung over."

"Hung over? I haven't had a hangover in centuries." Banon laughed. "The trick is to never stop drinking."

He chuckled heartily, pulling a tarnished flask from his jacket pocket and raising it in a salute before imbibing.

"I'll see you all at the ball," Angus called as Conner, Killian, and Banon waved, making their way out into the night.

"How about you?" Angus called as Patrick moved to pass him.

"I have a room at the hotels, but if you don't mind, I might take you up on your offer. It is late. I can just curl up in one of your snake baskets." He smiled.

"Believe it or not, my home does possess guest chambers."

"Excellent." Patrick smiled and followed Angus through a hallway on the opposite side of the room which led to a large dining room with several other hallways leading from it.

"This place reminds me of Darla's cave," Patrick mused.

"I know my house-keeping abilities are poor, but surely I am better than a dragon."

"Not by much." Patrick chuckled. Then, taking a calming breath, he became serious. "Angus, I have a question."

"Yes?" Angus turned to him.

"About the visions earlier. I see how the second and third visions are linked by the black-haired young woman, but what of the first?" Patrick asked. "It was a titan, wasn't it? The prophecies are coming true."

"I cannot pretend to know, but that girl's future is in some way entwined with their coming," Angus answered.

"If that is true, are you sure it is wise to aid her?"

"The old oak is not in the habit of giving visions. If it is interfering, it means our assistance is needed in some way."

Patrick sighed in heavy contemplation.

"Enough of prophecy, Brother." Angus insisted. "Let's think of the now."

"Like tomorrow's ball?"

"Like catching up with a nightcap. I have a wonderful fire jewel honeyed wine I've been saving since the early seventeen hundreds. I fear it might soon turn. Help me drink it?"

"How could I pass on such a gracious offer?" Patrick smiled, taking a seat at the large dining table.

"Excellent," Angus called as he went to a large cupboard filled to the brim with exotic decanters.

He pulled out a gold-colored bottle, two glasses, and brought them to the dining table. The two sat as he cracked open the bottle which emitted a sudden and brief burst of flame.

"Now," Angus called giving Patrick's glass an overly full pour. "Tell me more about this situation with Beau."

"We're going to need a second bottle for that."

The End

BIOGRAPHY OF A MADWOMAN

I was on the set of Christopher Guest's *Thank You for Your Consideration* when I realized I wanted to be a writer. My first novel was born of a long month sitting in a dusty studio with little to do. Let's just say that after a week of twelve-hour days, solitaire got pretty boring. That's when I decided to open my laptop and 'put to pen' the ideas and bizarre dreams rolling around in my head.

In San Diego, where I grew up, I first dreamt of Ithiria, a fantastic world where elementals guarded the natural balance and evil was born of good intentions. At Mesa College, where I studied theatre, the nuances of this land evolved into multiple stories mirroring our own world. While working in the film industry, the works of Grimm, Shelly, and other classic tales the world over came to exist on my pages in new forms. With ample 'set'time, I caught up on the reading I should have done while building sets at Madison High School. After winning the reality show **Search For The Next Elvira** and discovering the works of Christopher Moore, many of my characters took a comedic turn, with zombies who play soccer with each other's heads and witches saddled with cackling disorders.

It wasn't long until the creatures of Ithiria began to cross each other's stories. Life is an adventure and I believe this constant change should translate into one's work. Every year of attending Masquerade Balls, Steampunk events, and Comic Conventions causes my stories to become more fantastic. Each set I work on, from *I Love You, Man* to *Star Trek*, drives me to add new creations. What filters onto the page always surprises me.

I have a near-constant habit of nerding out on anything comic book, movie, myth, fairy tale, or supernatural, which has forced me to find ways to combine the things I love. So far, Ithiria has tales of unwitting royals who unearth great magic, children who wander into dark woods in search of dark creatures, vampires who discover their origins go deeper than a mere lifestyle change, and sheltered adolescents who find themselves capable of heroic feats. All of these plots and characters work toward the greater history of Ithiria; which as in our own world, is just the beginning.

SPECIAL THANKS!

A while ago I tried to raise funds via Indigogo so that I could afford to edit and publish my book. While most of the book has been Frankensteined together by the meager moneys I could put into it and with help from such amazing people as Eric Enroth, Travis Noble, and Naomi Gibson, there were also a few excellent people in Indigogo land who donated what they could to help get the book out. Your contributions have gone a long way toward reediting and rereleasing this book.

So, huge, huge, huge thank you to:

Lara Irving

Wayne Woodall

Carl Manko

Luis Esparza

Amy Judd Lieberman

I NEED YOUR HELP...

As an indie author, a large part of my success comes from the reviews I earn. If you enjoyed this book, please leave a review wherever you bought it.

To find out more, visit my site at aprilwahlin.com.

32729763R10121

Made in the USA
San Bernardino, CA
16 April 2016